THE TOSA DIARY

THE TOSA DIARY

TRANSLATED FROM THE JAPANESE
BY
WILLIAM N. PORTER

CHARLES E. TUTTLE CO.: PUBLISHERS
RUTLAND, VERMONT & TOKYO, JAPAN

Representatives

Continental Europe: BOXERBOOKS, INC., *Zurich*

British Isles: PRENTICE-HALL INTERNATIONAL, INC., *London*

Australasia: BOOK WISE (AUSTRALIA) PTY. LTD.
104-108 Sussex Street, Sydney 2000

Published by the Charles E. Tuttle Company, Inc.
of Rutland, Vermont & Tokyo, Japan
with editorial offices at
Suido 1-chome, 2-6, Bunkyo-ku, Tokyo, Japan

© *1981 by Charles E. Tuttle Co., Inc.*

Library of Congress Catalog Card No. 80-51194

International Standard Book No. 0-8048-1371-X

First Tuttle edition, 1981

PRINTED IN JAPAN

PUBLISHER'S FOREWORD

This early translation of a classic work of Japanese literature retains its charm more than half a century after initial publication in 1912, and it is a distinct satisfaction to present it once more for the pleasure of discerning readers. The appearance in later years of other English translations of the work has in no way diminished the value of this one, as all who appreciate writing of a truly engaging quality will recognize.

Although it has proven impossible for technical reasons to reproduce the sketch of Ki no Tsurayuki's route that appeared in the original edition, the *Tosa Diary* continues to provide the reader with a fascinating glimpse of tenth-century Japan, as well as a literary work of enduring stature. With his great experience in translating ancient Japanese poetry, William N. Porter was ideally equipped to render into English the elegant prose and many *tanka* poems in this book. The publisher takes more than the usual pleasure in offering his translation to the public.

INTRODUCTION

THE *Tosa Nikki*, or Tosa Diary, was written in the year A.D. 935 by Ki no Tsurayuki, a court nobleman of high rank, who died in 946. He had been appointed Governor of the Province of Tosa, in Shikoku, in 930, the first year of the reign of the Emperor Sujaku, and the diary is an account of his journey home by sea to Kyōto, which was then the capital. The total distance is only some 200 miles, but in those days it was considered no small undertaking, and took, as the diary shows, 55 days to accomplish; this period, however, covered several long stops on the way, including a 10 days' delay at Ōminato.

The boat used to convey such an important official would, no doubt, be of more than ordinary size, but there is nothing to tell us how large she was. A cabin is mentioned; but, though we are told that on one occasion a sail was hoisted, they relied chiefly upon oars as a means of propulsion, for sails in those early days were but seldom used. They travelled very leisurely, camping each night upon shore, and remaining there the next day if the weather looked at all threatening. Mr. H. A. C. Bonar's investigations on the subject of early Japanese shipping, as given in his paper read before the Asiatic Society of Japan in 1887, supply little or no information for this early period. He mentions an old canoe which was dug out near Ōsaka (the ancient port of Naniwa) in the year 1878 and is now shown in the permanent exhibition of that city. Its date could not be ascertained with any certainty, but it was estimated to be over 1000 years old, which would carry it back approximately to the period of the Tosa Diary; and Tsurayuki's ship might very well have been something like it. Its shape is that of a large hollowed out trunk of a tree, its length is 37ft. 5 in., and greatest width 4ft. 8in.

Ki no Tsurayuki was famous as a writer both of prose and poetry. Between the years 905 and 922 he, with assistance from others, compiled the *Kokinshū*, a famous collection of early Japanese poetry, to which he contributed a preface, which is much admired for its literary though somewhat flowery style. The Tosa Diary, which also ranks high among the literature of Old Japan, is, however, written in a very different tone. The English reader will no doubt be struck by its artless simplicity and quiet humour, which is as welcome as it is unexpected from a Japanese nobleman of the tenth century. His sufferings from sea-sickness, his grief for the loss of his mirror, his pride when his little daughter composes a verse in reply to that made by a visitor whom he evidently dislikes, the endless verses of his own that he cannot resist quoting, and the way in which he depreciates the verses of others, as well as many other details, supply a very human touch to the diary.

A characteristic feature of his style is the contrast of words he introduces; such as, he 'sang a song of the East, though he was still in the Land of the West', and 'his feelings were somewhat calmed, although the sea was still very rough', &c. The late Dr. Aston in his *History of Japanese Literature* writes: 'The *Tosa Nikki* is a striking example of the importance of style. It contains no exciting adventures or romantic situations; there are in it no wise maxims or novel information; its only merit is that it describes in simple yet elegant language, and with a vein of playful humour, the ordinary life of a traveller in Japan at the time when it was written. But this has proved sufficient to give it a high rank amongst Japanese classics, and has ensured its being handed down to our own day·as a most esteemed model for composition in the native Japanese style. It has been followed by many imitations, but has had no equal.'

The Japanese language as usually written is a combination of ideographic and phonetic characters, but Tsurayuki opens his diary by announcing that he intends to write it only in phonetics. As these were comparatively simple to learn, while a knowledge of the ideographs involved a profound study of the classical Chinese language, the former became known as ' the women's language ' and the latter as ' the men's language '. Tsurayuki, therefore, in order to justify his use of phonetics only, writes the diary in the character of a woman and mentions himself only in the third person, which adds considerably to the difficulties of the translator. He also calls himself by many different names, such as *yuku hito* (the traveller), *funagimi* (the passenger), but oftenest simply *aru hito* (a certain personage). To assist the English reader, I have put in inverted commas such of these names as are supposed to indicate the writer himself.

It is not known why he decided to dispense with ideographs and to use phonetics only, which at the time had been in use for barely a hundred years; possibly it was for the sake of simplicity, and to enable the less educated to read his work. The Japanese commentators say that his rather cowardly dread of meeting the pirates and his excessive grief for his dead child would have been inconsistent with anything but a female writer. On the other hand, Tsurayuki may have emphasized these two features so as to give an artistic finish to a diary which is supposed to be written by a woman.

With regard to the numerous verses quoted, they are all, with the exception of the two ' boat songs ', written in the

classical *tanka* metre, which was limited
to 5 lines and 31 syllables (5–7–5–7–7).
The making of verses has always been one
of the polite accomplishments in Japan,
and Tsurayuki seldom misses an opportunity of composing. In the translation
I have retained the original metre, and
introduced a rhyme in the last couplet
to emphasize the caesura between the
third and fourth lines of the Japanese. It
is a wellnigh hopeless task to attempt
a translation of Japanese verses, which,
while retaining the metre, is true to the
original both in spirit and in letter, and it
would not be fair to the illustrious poet
to judge his work by the English version
as given here. Perhaps I may paraphrase
Tsurayuki as follows : ' People who read
it will say to themselves that this kind of
stuff is very poor. But the translator
produced it with a good deal of difficulty,
so they should stop whispering such cruel
things about it.'

Owing to the change of calendar the dates as given in the diary are apt to lead one astray, and I have therefore given the corresponding date in the Gregorian calendar for each entry.

The accompanying sketch of the route taken by Ki no Tsurayuki is only approximately correct, for it is not possible at this date to identify with certainty all the places named in the diary. Most of those marked on the sketch were taken from an excellent map of Japan in the possession of the Hydrographic Department of the Admiralty, which I was permitted to consult, and only one or two in addition to the four unnamed stopping-places are conjectures.

I should like to record here my grateful thanks to Mr. Choichi Fujino and to Major H. Haraguchi for their kind assistance in some of the more difficult passages.

W. N. P.

Oitaru wo, chichi to se-yo.

(Japanese Proverb.)

That which is old should be treated with the
respect due to a father.

TOSA NIKKI

*Otoko mo su to iu, Nikki to iu mono wo,
onna mo shite min tote suru nari.*

A. D. 935.

28 JAN. Sore no toshi, shiwasu no
hatsuka amari hito hi no hi no Inu no
Toki ni kado desu. Sono yoshi, isasaka
mono ni kaki-tsuku. Aru hito, agata no
yo-tose itsu-tose hatete, rei no koto-domo,
mina, shioete, geyu nado torite, sumu
tachi-yori-idete, fune ni noru-beki tokoro
e wataru. Kore kare, shiru shiranu
okurisu. Toshi-goro yoku gushitsuru hito-
bito nan, wakare gataku omoite, sono hi,

THE TOSA DIARY

It is generally a man who writes what is called a Diary, but now a woman will see what she can do.[1]

A.D. 935.

28 JAN. One year on the twenty-first day of the twelfth month 'a certain personage' left home at the Hour of the Dog (8.0 p.m.), which was the beginning of this modest record. He had just completed the usual period of four or five years as Governor of a Province; everything had been wound up, documents, &c., had been handed over, and now he was about to go down to the place of embarkation; for he was to travel on shipboard. All sorts of people, both friends and strangers, came to see him off, including many who had served him faithfully during the past

shikiri ni, tokaku shitsutsu nonoshiru uchi
ni yo fukenu.

29 JAN. *Nijū ni nichi*, Izumi no Kuni
made, tairaka ni to negai tatsu. Fujiwara
no Tokisane, funaji naredo, uma no
hanamuke su. Kami, naka, shimo, yei
sugite, ito ayashiku, shio umi no hotori
nite, azare aeri.

30 JAN. *Nijū san nichi*, Yagi no Yasunori to iu hito ari. Kono hito, Kuni ni
kanarazushimo ide tsukawaruru mono ni
arazu. Kore zo, tadashiki yō nite, uma
no hanamuke shitaru. Mamori gara ni
ya aran. Kuni-bito no kokoro no tsune
to shite, ima wa tote, miezu naru wo,
kokoro aru mono wa, hajizu ni nan ki

years, and who sorrowed at the thought
of losing him that day. There was endless bustle and confusion; and so with one
thing and another the night drew on.

29 JAN. 22nd day.—He prayed for
a calm voyage to the Land of Izumi.
Fujiwara no Tokisané came to ' turn his
horse's head ',[2] although he was to travel
by sea. Upper, middle, and lower classes
all drank too heavily, and, wonderful to
relate, there they were on the edge of the
salt sea itself all useless and incompetent ![3]

30 JAN. 23rd day.—A certain man,
called Yagi no Yasunori, although he was
of too high rank to have been one of his
regular attendants in the Province, openly
made him a farewell present. Perhaps
he had not made a very good Governor ;
but still, the country-folk usually on an
occasion like this just said good-bye, and
then disappeared ; and here was a kind

keru. Kore wa, mono ni yorite, homuru
ni shimo arazu.

31 JAN. *Nijū yokka*, Kōshi, uma no
hanamuke ni idemaseri. Ari-to-aru, kami-
shimo, warawa made, yoi shirete, hito
moji wo dani shiranu mono shiga, ashi
wa, tomoji ni fumite zo asobu.

1 FEB. *Nijū go nichi*, Mori no Tachi
yori, yobi ni, fumi mote-kitareri. Yo-
barete itarite. Hi hito hi, yo hito yo,
tokaku, asobu yō nite, ake ni keri.

2 FEB. *Nijū roku nichi*, nao, Mori no
Tachi nite, aruji shi nonoshirite, onoko-
ra made ni, mono kazuketari. Kara uta,

heart which was not ashamed to come back again. This word of praise for him is not due to the present he brought !

31 JAN. 24*th day.*—The Chief Priest made him a farewell present ; and accordingly everybody, high and low, even the very boys, got so intoxicated, that those who did not know how to write one word found that their feet had playfully trodden the word ' ten ' in the sand.[4]

1 FEB. 25*th day.*—A written invitation arrived from Government House,[5] asking him to go and call. He accordingly went to call ; and, what with one thing and another, all day and all night passed away pleasantly, till at last the day broke.

2 FEB. 26*th day.*—Still at Government House, where the entertainment grew boisterous ; the host and even the servants became uproarious. With loud voices

koye agete ii keri. Yamato uta, aruji mo, marōdo mo, koto hito mo ii aeri keri. Kara uta wa, kore ni wa kakazu. Yamato uta, aruji no Mori no yomeri keru.

Miyako idete
Kimi ni awan to
Koshi mono wo
Koshi kai mo naku
Wakarenuru kana.

To nan ari kereba, kaeru saki no Kami no yomeru.

Shirotae no
Nami-ji wo tōku
Yuki-kaite
Ware ni ni-beki wa
Tare naranaku ni.

Koto hito-bito no mo ari keredo, sakashiki mo nakaru-beshi. Tokaku iite, saki no Kami mo, ima no mo, morotomo ni orite, ima no aruji mo, saki no mo, te

Chinese poems were declaimed ; and the
host, ' the visitor' and the other guests
recited Japanese verses.   The Chinese
poems are not recorded here ;[6] but the
following is the Japanese verse composed
by the Governor, as host :

> From the Capital
> Far across the sea I came,
>   Came to see my Lord ;
> But alas ! 'twas all in vain,
> For we now must part again.

Whereupon ' the former Governor'
composed this in reply :

> I, too, travelled far
> O'er the stormy road of waves
>   White with crested foam ;
> Scarce, I think, another man
> Would have faced the risks we ran !

There were also verses composed by
many others, but they were quite worth-
less. Having recited these, the late and

tori-kawashite, ei-goto ni, kokochi yoge
naru koto shite, ide ni keri.

3 FEB. *Nijū shichi nichi*, Ōtsu yori,
Urato wo sashite kogi-izu. Kaku aru
uchi ni, Miyako nite umaretarishi onna
go, Kuni nite niwaka ni use ni shikaba,
konogoro no ide-tachi isogi wo miredo,
nani-koto mo e iwazu. Miyako e kaeru
ni, onna go no naki nomi zo kanashimi
kōru. Aru hito-bito mo e taezu. Kono
ma ni aru hito no kakite, idaseru uta.

> Miyako e to
> Omou mo mono no
> Kanashiki wa
> Kaeranu hito no
> Areba nari keri.

the present Governors descended together; the present and the late hosts went forth hand in hand, in good fellowship and the best of spirits.

3 FEB. *27th day.*—They started from Ōtsu and began to row to Urato. His little daughter,[7] who had been born in the Capital, had died a short time previously in the Province very suddenly ; and now, when, as we see, he was departing in haste, what was he to say ! All his love was changed to grief, for he will now have no little daughter to return with him to the Capital. It was more than most men could bear ; but in this case ' a certain personage ' dragged out the following verse :

> Though I now return
> To my home, the Capital,
>   Sad it is to think
> One for whom I mourn in vain
> Never will return again.

Mata, aru toki ni wa,

> Aru mono to
> Wasure-tsutsu nao
> Naki hito wo
> Izura to tou zo
> Kanashi-kari keru.

To ii keru ma ni. Kago no Saki to iu tokoro ni, Kami no harakara, mata, koto hito, kore kare, sake nado mote ōi-kite, iso ni ori-ite, wakare-gataki koto wo iu. Kami no Tachi no hito-bito no uchi ni, kono kuru hito-bito zo, kokoro aru yō ni iware honomeku. Kaku, wakare-gataku iite, kano hito-bito no kuchi-ami mo moro mochi nite, kono umibe nite, ninai idaseru uta.

> Oshi to omou
> Hito ya tomaru to
> Ashi kamo no

He composed the following also upon the same occasion :

> Could I e'er forget
> What is past, I still should grieve
> If she were not here ;
> Seeking for her, I should say,
> ' Where's my little girl to-day ? '

Such were his words. At a place named Cape Kago the Governor's brother,[8] some strangers and many others hurried down to the shore with *saké* and other good things to bid a sad farewell ; and all the people from Government House, who had come here, spoke softly in the kindness of their hearts. To express their grief at parting, these good people clustered together upon the sea-shore and dragged out the following verse,—which was as heavy as a net full of fishes !

> Like a flock of ducks [9]
> Here among the reeds are we ;
> Deeply we regret

Uchi-murete koso
Ware wa ki ni kere.

Kakute ari kereba, ito itaku medete,
yuku hito no yomeri keru.

Sao sasedo
Sokoi mo shiranu
Wadatsumi no
Fukaki kokoro wo
Kimi ni miru kana.

To iu aida ni, kajitori. Mono no aware
mo shirade, onore-shi sake wo kurai tsureba,
hayaku inan tote, shio michinu. Kaze
mo fukinu-beshi to, sawakeba, fune ni
norinan to su. Kono ori ni, aru hito-
bito, orifushi ni tsukete, Kara uta-domo,
toki ni nitsu-kawashiki wo iu. Mata, aru
hito, Sai-Koku naredo, Kai-uta nado
utau. Kaku utau ni, funa-yakata no
chiri mo chiri, sora yuku kumo mo

Thy departure, and we would
Keep thee with us, if we could.

On this ' the traveller ' with the greatest
appreciation replied :

Sounding with my pole
Bottom is there none ; and thus
Like the Sea-God's realm,
Bottomless my loving heart,
When I think we now must part.

The steersman,[10] who had himself been
freely eating and drinking *saké* while all
this was going on, now remorselessly said
they must get away at once ; for the tide
was full, and he feared the wind might
blow and they would have a rough tossing
in the ship. Just about this time several
others wrote appropriate verses ; they
were Chinese poems and I have no doubt
they were worthy of the occasion ; ' a
certain personage ' also sang a song of the
East,[11]—though he was still in the Land

tadayoinu to zo iu naru. Koyoi, Urato ni tomaru Fujiwara no Tokisane, Tachibana no Suehira, koto hito-bito oi-kitari.

4 FEB. *Nijū hachi nichi*, Urato yori kogi-idete, Ōminato wo ou. Kono aida ni, hayaku no Kami no ko, Yamaguchi no Chimine, sake, yoki-mono-domo mote kite, fune ni iretari. Yuku-yuku nomi kuu.

5 FEB. *Nijū ku nichi*, Ōminato ni tomareri. Kusushi, furi-haete, toso, byaku-san, sake, kuwaete mote kitari. Kokoro-zashi aru ni nitari.

of the West. While these verses were being sung, we are told, even the dust in the cabin began to blow about and the clouds to scud across the sky! That evening a stop was made at Urato, to which spot Fujiwara no Tokisané and Tachibana no Suehira followed.[12]

4 FEB. 28*th day*.—They set out rowing from Urato and made for Ōminato, where Yamaguchi no Chiminé, the son of a former Governor, came with *saké* and good things to eat, which he put aboard the boat. There will be plenty to eat and drink during the voyage !

5 FEB. 29*th day*.—They remained at Ōminato, and the Doctor paid a visit, in order to present some spiced *saké* and *byakusan* appropriate to the season, as well as ordinary *saké* ; [13] this he did from pure kindness of heart.

6 FEB. *Gwanjitsu,* nao onaji tomari nari. Byakusan wo aru-mono, yo no ma tote, funa-yakata ni sashihasameri kereba, kaze ni fuki narasasete, umi ni irete, e nomazu narinu, imo mo arame mo, haga-tame mo nashi. Kayō no mono mo naki kuni nari. Motomeshi mo okazu. Tada, oshiayu no kuchi wo nomi zo suu. Kono suu hito-bito no kuchi wo, oshiayu, moshi, omou yō aran ya. Kyō wa, Miyako nomi zo omoi-yararuru. Kokonoye no Kado no shirikumenawa no, nayoshi no kashira, hihira kira, ikani to zo ii aeru.

7 FEB. *Futsuka,* nao Ōminato ni toma-reri. Kōshi mono sake okosetari.

6 FEB. *New Year's Day.*—Still they remained at the same place. The *byakusan* had been placed for safe-keeping during the night in the ship's cabin ; but the wind which is usual at this time of year got up and blew it all into the sea. They had nothing left to drink, no potatoes, no seaweed and no rice-cakes ; the neighbourhood could supply nothing of this kind, and so their wants could not be satisfied. They could do nothing more than suck the head of a trout. What must the trout have thought of everybody sucking it in turn ! That day he could think of nothing but the Capital, and talk of nothing but the straw rope stretched across the Gates of the Imperial Palace, the mullet heads and the holly.[14]

7 FEB. *2nd day.*—Still at Ōminato. The Chief Priest sent a gift of food and *saké.*

8 FEB. *Mikka*, onaji tokoro nari. Moshi, kaze nami no shibashi to oshimu kokoro ya aran. Kokoro mo to nashi.

9 FEB. *Yokka*, kaze fukeba, e ide-tatazu. Masatsura, sake yoki-mono tatematsureri. Kōyō no mono mote kuru hito ni, nao-shi-mo e arade, isasakewaza sesasu mono mo nashi. Nigiwawashiki yō naredo, makuru kokochi su.

10 FEB. *Itsuka*, kaze nami yamaneba, nao, onaji tokoro ni ari. Hito-bito taezu toburai-niku.

11 FEB. *Muika*, kino no gotoshi.

8 FEB. *3rd day.*—In the same place. I wonder if the wind and waves had a tender feeling for him, as they seemed to wish to delay him for some time? He certainly had no tender feeling for them!

9 FEB. *4th day.*—No start was made, as a high wind was still blowing. Masatsura presented a gift of *saké* and other good things. A man who came with presents like this ought not to have come in vain ; but there was literally nothing to offer him ; and, though it all looked lively enough, his spirits were very low.

10 FEB. *5th day.*—As the wind and waves had not gone down, they still remained at the same spot, and many people constantly came to call upon him.

11 FEB. *6th day*, is the same as yesterday.

12 FEB. *Nanuka* ni narinu. Onaji minato ni ari. Kyō wa, Ao Uma wo omoedo, kainashi. Tada, nami no shiroki nomi zo miyuru. Kakaru ma ni, hito no ie no Ike to na aru tokoro yori, koi wa nakute, funa yori hajimete, kawa no mo, umi no mo koto mono wo mo, nagabitsu ni ninai tsuzukete, okosetari. Wakana ko ni irete, kiji nado hana ni tsuketari. Wakana zo, kyō wo shirasetaru. Uta ari, sono uta,

Asajiu no
Nobe nishi areba
Mizu mo naki
Ike ni tsumitsuru
Wakana nari keri.

Ito okashi. Kono Ike to iu wa, tokoro no na nari. Yoki hito no, otoko ni tsukite,

12 FEB. The *7th day* came and found them still at the same port. This day his thoughts were fixed upon the Festival of the Grey Horse ; [15] but it was of no good wishing for that, for all he could see were the white waves. About this time a present arrived from somebody's estate which was called Iké ; [16] a long box slung from a pole containing, not carp, but many other kinds of river and sea fish, beginning with goldfish ; also green vegetables packed in a basket, pheasants, game, and flowers. The green vegetables[17] reminded him what day it was, for they bore the following verse :

> Water is there none
> On the wild and lonely moor
> Where the rushes grow ;
> But from Iké, see, we bring
> Fresh green shoots of early spring.

A very amusing verse. This estate called Iké, he was told, was occupied by

kudarite, sumi-keru nari. Kono nagabitsu no mono wa, mina, hito, warawa
made ni kuretareba. Aki michite, funago-
domo wa, hara tsuzumi-uchite, umi wo
sae odorokashite, nami wo mo tatetsu-
beshi. Kakute. Kono ma ni koto
ōkari. Kyō, warigo motasete kitaru
hito, sono na nado zo ya. Ima omoi-
iden. Kono hito, uta yoman to omou
kokoro arite nari keri. To kaku ii-iite,
nami no tatsu naru koto to uree iite,
yomeru uta.

　　　Yukusaki ni
　　　Tatsu shira nami no
　　　Koye yori mo
　　　Okurete nakan
　　　Ware ya masaran.

a lady of rank, who had come down from the Capital and who lived there with her husband. The contents of the long box were distributed among all, even the boys were not forgotten ; they all had abundance to eat, and the sailors patted their bellies contentedly. The sea was so shocked at the sight, that the waves began to get up, and while this was going on many things happened. This day a man arrived with a servant carrying a box of food ; what *was* his name ? Perhaps I shall think of it soon. Well, this man had it in his mind that he would compose a poem. He talked about it a good deal, and then, taking as his subject the sad sight of the waves getting up, composed this :

On thy journey hence,
Though the billows white with spray
Ever louder roar,
When to thee ' Farewell ' I call,
My cries shall surpass them all.

To zo yomeru, ito ō koye naru-beshi.
Mote kitaru mono yori wa, uta wa ikaga
aran. Kono uta wo, kore kare awaregare-
domo, hitori mo kaeshi sezu. Shitsu-beki
hito mo majireredo, kore wo nomi
itagari, mono wo nomi kuite yo fukenu.
Kono utanushi mata makarazu to iite,
tachinu. Aru hito no ko no warawa naru,
hisoka ni iu. ' Maro, kono uta no kaeshi
sen ' to iu. Odorokite, ito okashiki koto
kana. Yomiten yawa, yomitsu-beku wa,
haya iyekashi to iu ni, makarazu tote,
tachinuru hito wo machite yoman to,
motome keru wo, yo fukenu to niya
ari-ken. Yagate ini-keri. Somo-somo.
Ikaga yomitaru to, ibukashigarite tou.

Well, that was his verse. He must
surely have had a very loud voice, and
his poem was hardly as good as what he
brought. Every one sympathized with this
verse, but nobody composed one in reply ;
and, though there were many there who
could have done so, they merely bore it in
silence. And so with eating and drinking
the night drew on, till the poet got up
and went off, promising to come back
again. ' A certain personage's ' little
child [18] whispered, ' I will make a verse in
reply to his.' What a surprise ! and how
very amusing ! You can't compose a
verse ! If you think you can, please let us
have it at once. She waited a moment
for the man who had gone out and had
promised to return, and then went to
look for him ; but the night had grown
late, and he did not come back. Mean-
while we asked ourselves doubtfully, what
kind of verse this would be. The child
was shy and unwilling to give it, but

Kono warawa, sasuga ni, hajite iwazu.
Shiite toeba, ieru uta.

> Yuku hito mo
> Tomaru mo sode no
> Namida gawa
> Migiwa nomi koso
> Nure-masari kere.

To nan yomeru. Kaku wa iu mono ka.
Utsukushi kereba niya aran. Ito omowazu
nari. Warawa goto nite wa, nanika wa
sen. Onna, okina ni wo shitsu-beshi.
Ashiku mo are. Ikani mo are. Tayori
araba, yaran tote, okarenu-meri.

13 FEB. *Yōka*, sawaru koto arite, nao,
onaji tokoro nari. Koyoi no tsuki wa,
umi ni zo iru. Kore wo mite, Narihira
no Kimi no

> 'Yama no ha nigete
> Irezu mo aranan.'

when spoken to firmly she repeated this :

See, the shore is wet
With the stream of tears which pours
From the sleeves of those
Who upon the beach must stay,
Or who go upon their way.

That was her verse. How clever of her to get an idea like that ! I did not think she could have done it. How could a mere child do so well ? It is worthy of a woman or an old man. Well, whether it is poor, or whatever it is, it shall be carefully preserved, in case there may be an opportunity to send it to the poet.

13 FEB. *8th day.*—Something or other was wrong, and they still remained where they were. That evening the moon sank into the sea. The poet Narihira once watched the setting moon and sang :

' Would the hills but fly away
Longer might the moonlight stay.' [19]

To iu uta nan oboyuru. Moshi, umibe
nite yomamashigaba,

> Nami tachi-saete
> Irezu mo aranan.

To yomite mashi ya. Ima, kono uta
wo omoi-idete, aru hito no yomeri keru.

> Teru tsuki no
> Nagaruru mireba
> Ama no Gawa
> Izuru minato wa
> Umi ni zari keru.

To ya.

14 FEB. *Kokonoka*, tsutomete, Ōminato
yori Nawa no tomari wo owan tote
kogi-ide keri. Korekare, tagai ni (Kuni
no sakai no uchi wa) tote mi-okuri ni
kuru hito, amata ga naka ni, Fujiwara no

If the poet, when he composed this, had been on the sea-shore, he would no doubt have written :

Would the waves but bar the way
Longer might the moonlight stay.

Meditating still upon the verse, ' a certain personage ' composed this :

Forward sails the moon
On the River of the Sky [20]
    Shining overhead ;
Like the lovely moon may we
Leave this port and put to sea.

There !

14 FEB. *9th day*.—They set out from Ōminato the first thing in the morning and rowed on, intending to stop at Nawa. All united in coming to bid him farewell (now that they were passing the boundaries of the Province) ; among many others, Fujiwara no Tokisané,

Tokisane, Tachibana no Suehira, Hasabe no Yukimasa ra nan, On Yakata yori ideta-maishi hi yori, kokokashiko ni oikuru. Kono hito-bito zo, kokoro-zashi aru hito nari keru. Kono hito-bito no fukaki kokoro-zashi wa, kono umi ni mo otorazaru-beshi. Kore yori, ima wa kogi hanarete yuku. Kore wo mi-okuran tote zo, kono hito-domo wa, oiki keru. Kakute kogi-yuku mani-mani, umi no hotori ni todomaru hito mo tōku narinu. Fune no hito mo miezu narinu. Kishi ni mo iu koto aru-beshi. Fune ni mo omou koto aredo, kai-nashi. Kakaredo, kono uta wo, hitorigoto ni shite yaminu.

> Omoiyaru
> Kokoro wa umi wo
> Wataredomo
> Fumishi nakereba
> Shirazu ya aruran.

Tachibana no Suehira, and Hasabé no Yukimasa, &c. From the day he left his Official Residence, people all the way along the route had come to see him off, and they all did it from kindness of heart ; in fact, their kind hearts seemed to be as bottomless as the sea. At this spot, then, they parted and rowed on, for it was here that these people had come to see him off. After this, as they rowed gently forward, those who remained upon the sea-shore grew further and further away, and they in their turn could no longer see those in the boat ; from the shore they could not speak to the ship, and, if the ship called to them, it was all in vain. This being so, he could only recite the following verse to himself :

> Far across the sea
> In my heart I fly to you
>   Bidding you farewell ;
> But no written word, alas !
> From the ship to you may pass.

Kakute, Uta no matsubara wo yuki-sugu. Sono matsu no kazu ikusobaku, iku chitose hetari to shirazu. Moto goto ni nami uchi-yose, eda goto ni tsuru zo tobikō, omoshiroshi to miru ni taezu shite, funabito no yomeru uta.

Mi-wataseba
Matsu no ure goto ni
Sumu tsuru wa
Chiyo no dochi to zo
Omou-bera naru.

To ya. Kono uta wa, tokoro wo miru ni e masarazu. Kaku aru wo mi-tsutsu kogi-yuku mani-mani, yama mo umi mo mina kure, yo fukete, nishi higashi mo miezu shite, teke no koto, kajitori no kokoro ni makasetsu. Otoko mo narawanu wa, ito mo kokorobososhi. Mashite, onna

After this they passed the pine forest
of Uta. I know not how many pine trees
there were there, nor for how many
thousand years they had lived.[21] The
ripples lapped against the foot of each,
and amid the branches of each the storks
flitted about. Overcome by such a
charming prospect ' the seafarer ' composed this :

On the shore the storks
Perched amid the pine tree tops
Charm my oving gaze ;
For a thousand years, I ween,
Storks and pines fast friends have been.

There ! And the song is no more lovely
than was the prospect. Still admiring the
beautiful scene, they rowed gently forward ; mountains and sea all became dim,
and the night drew on. As he could no
longer distinguish east from west, he left
all thought about the weather to the steersman. Those of the men who were unused

wa funazoko ni kashira wo tsuki-atete, ne
wo nomi zo naku, kaku omoedo, funago,
kajitori wa, funa-uta utaite, nani to mo
omoerazu. Sono utau uta,—

> Haru no no nite zo,
> Ne woba naku,
> Waga susuki nite,
> Te wo kiru-kiru,
> Tsundaru na wo,
> Oya mahoruran,
> Shūtome ya kūran,
> Kaeraya,
> Yombe no na wo,
> Soragoto wo shite,
> Oginori waza wo shite,
> Zeni mo mote kozu,
> Onore dani kozu.

Kore narazu ōkaredo, kakazu. Korera
wo, hito no warau wo kikite, umi wa

to the sea began to feel gloomy and pensive, while the women laid their heads upon the bottom of the boat and cried aloud. But the steersman and sailors thought nothing of it all and sang their boat song ; this is it :

> In the fields this fine spring day
>   I have cut my hand
> With the long grass growing there,
>   And I cry aloud
>   As I pick the greens ;
> Endless is my parent's greed,
> But my mother must I feed.
>   And, when I go home,
>   Those I picked last night,—
> They were pilfered by a thief,
> One who took the greens on tick
> Leaving not a cent, alack !
> And he has not yet come back.[22]

There was a good deal more of this sort of thing, but I will not record it. On hearing the others laughing at it,

aruredo, kokoro wa sukoshi naginu. Kaku yuki kurashite, tomari ni itarite, okina hito hitori, tōme hitori, aru ga naka ni, kokochi ashimi shite, mono mo monoshi tamawade, hisomarinu.

15 FEB. *Tōka*, kyō wa, kono Nawa no tomari ni tomarinu.

16 FEB. *Jū ichi nichi*, akatsuki ni fune wo idashite, Murotsu wo ou. Hito mina, mada netareba, umi no arisama mo miezu. Tada, tsuki wo mite zo, nishi higashi woba shiri keru. Kakaru ma ni, mina yo akete, te arai, rei no kotodomo shite, hiru ni narinu. Imashi, Hane to iu tokoro ni tsukinu. Wakaki warawa, kono tokoro no na wo kikite, Hane to iu wa, tori no hane no yō ni ya aru to iu. Mada wakaki warawa no koto nareba, hito-bito warau ni,

his feelings were somewhat calmed, although the sea was still very rough. It
was now quite dark as they rowed forward,
and on getting to their stopping-place
' a solitary old man ' and a solitary old
woman among all the others, feeling unwell, took no food and retired to rest.[23]

15 FEB. 10*th day*.—To-day they remained at this stopping-place, Nawa.

16 FEB. 11*th day*.—The boat started
at break of day and headed for Murotsu.
They were all still half asleep, and accordingly took no notice of the condition of
the sea. But the position of the moon
indicated which was east and which was
west, and so the day gradually became
light. They washed their hands, performed their toilets, and by that time
it was noon. At last they arrived at a
place called Hané.[24] A little child, on hearing the name of the place, asked if Hané
got its name from the wings of a bird ;

ari keru onna warawa nan, kono uta wo yomeru.

> Makoto nite
> Na ni kiku tokoro
> Hane naraba
> Tobu ga gotoku ni
> Miyako e mogana.

To zo ieru. Otoko mo onna mo, ikade toku Miyako e mogana to omou kokoro areba, kono uta yoshi to ni wa aranedo, geni to omoite, hito-bito wasurezu. Kono Hane to iu tokoro tou warawa no tsuide ni zo, mata, mukashi no hito wo omoi-idete, izure no toki ni ka wasururu. Kyō wa, mashite, haha no kanashimu koto wa, kudarishi toki no hito no kazu taraneba, furuki uta ni,

> ' Kazu wa tarade zo
> Kaeru-bera naru.'

and, while they were all laughing at such
a childish question, a little girl composed
this verse :

> If this place Hané
> Chance to have a pair of wings,
>   As its name implies,
> May they help us in our need
> To the Capital with speed.

So she spoke. And, though it may
not be a very good verse, everybody,
men and women alike, who really wished
in their hearts for a speedy voyage to the
Capital, pondered it over and kept it in
mind. This child's question about the spot
called Hané again reminded him of one who
was gone. When will she ever be forgotten!
Her mother, too, grieved to-day more than
ever, and quoted an old verse to the effect
that there is one missing out of those who
went down from the Capital :

> ' Was there in the flock last year
>   One who does not reappear ? ' [25]

To iu koto wo omoi-idete, hito no yomeru.

>Yo no naka ni
>Omoi aredo mo
>Ko wo kōru
>Omoi ni masaru
>Omoi naki kana.

To ii-tsutsu nan.

17 FEB. *Jū ni nichi*, ame furazu. Fumitoki, Koremochi ga fune no, oku-retarishi, Narashitsu yori Murotsu ni tsukinu.

18 FEB. *Jū san nichi*, akatsuki ni, isa-saka ame furu. Shibashi arite yaminu. Otoko, onna, korekare yuami nado sen tote, atari no yoroshiki tokoro ni orite yuku, umi wo miyareba,

>Kumo mo mina
>Nami to zo miyuru

Thinking over these words, ' somebody '
composed this :

> In the midst of life
> Cares in plenty though there be,
> Yet the little child
> Whom I loved beyond compare
> Was by far my greatest care.[26]

And thus he expressed his feelings.

17 FEB. 12*th day*.—The rain stopped,
and the boat containing Fumitoki and
Koremochi, who had been left behind,
arrived at Murotsu from Narashitsu.

18 FEB. 13*th day*.—The rain was gently
falling at daybreak, but it soon stopped,
and then men and women together went
down to a suitable place in the vicinity
and had a hot bath.[27] Looking out over
the sea, he composed this verse :

> Overhead the clouds
> Look to me like rippling waves ;

Ama mogana
Izure ka umi to
Toite shiru-beku.

To nan uta yomeru. Sate tōka amari nareba, tsuki omoshiroshi. Fune ni nori someshi hi yori, fune ni wa, kurenai koku, yoki kinu kizu, sore wa, Umi no Kami ni ojite to ii, [nani no ashi kage ni kotozukete, hoya no tsuma no izushi, sushi, awabi wo zo, kokoro ni mo arane, hagi ni agete mise akeru.]

19 FEB. *Jū yokka*, akatsuki yori ame fureba, onaji tokoro ni tomareri. Funagimi sechimi su. Sōjimono nakereba, Uma no Toki yori nochi ni, kajitori no, kinō tsuritarishi tai ni, zeni nakereba, yone wo tori-kakete, ochirarenu. Kakaru koto ōku arinu. Kajitori, mata, tai mote

Were the fishers here,
' Which is sea, and which is sky ? '
I would ask, and they'd reply.

Well, as it was after the tenth day, the moon was particularly beautiful. All these days, since first he set foot aboard ship, he had never worn his handsome bright scarlet costume, because he feared to offend the God of the Sea ; [28] yet . . .

19 FEB. 14*th day*.—Rain was falling at daybreak, so they remained where they were. ' The passenger ' was fasting, and, though it was now past the Hour of the Horse (noon), he had not even taken any vegetable food. But the steersman on the previous day had caught a bream ; so having no coppers he successfully negotiated some rice for it. This transaction was often repeated, and he frequently traded rice and *saké*,

kitari, yone, sake, shibashiba kuru. Kajitori keshiki ashikarazu.

20 **FEB.** *Jū go nichi*, kyō, azuki kayu
nizu. Kuchi-oshiku, nao, hi no ashikereba,
izaru hodo ni zo, kyō, hatsuka amari
henuru. Itazura ni, hi wo okureba,
hito-bito, umi wo nagame-tsutsu zo aru
onna no warawa no ieru.

Tateba tatsu
Ireba mata iru
Fuku kaze to
Nami to wa omou
Dochi ni ya aruran.

Iugainaki mono no ieru ni wa, ito
nitsukawashi.

21 **FEB.** *Jū roku nichi*, kaze nami yamaneba, nao, onaji tokoro ni tomareri.

whenever the steersman happened to catch bream ; and the latter's countenance became quite jovial in consequence.

20 FEB. 15*th day.*—This day no rice and bean gruel was cooked, and, as it was an unlucky day, they crawled slowly along, much to his regret.[29]   To-day the voyage had already lasted more than twenty days, and they were but as so many days wasted. While all were gazing out to sea, a little girl recited this :

When the breezes drop
Quickly do the waves subside,
  When the wind gets up
Then the waves again arise ;
Comrade-like they sympathize.

This is, no doubt, hardly worth giving, but it is very appropriate.

21 FEB. 16*th day.*—As the wind and waves had not gone down, they remained

Tada, ' Umi ni nami naku shite, itsushika mi saki to iu tokoro wataran ' to nomi nan omou wo, kaze nami tomo ni yamu-beku mo arazu, aru hito no, kono nami tatsu wo mite, yomeru uta,

> Shimo dani mo
> Okanu kata zo to
> Iu naredo
> Nami no naka ni wa
> Yuki zo furi keru.

Sate fune ni norishi hi yori, kyō made wa, hatsuka amari itsuka ni nari ni keri.

22 FEB. *Jū shichi nichi*, kumoreru kumo nakunarite, akatsuki tsukiyo ito omoshiro-kereba, fune wo idashite kogi-yuku. Kono ma ni, kumo no ue mo,

where they were.   He could think of
nothing but, ' When will these wind-blown
waves subside, so that we may weather
this terrible headland ? '   However, as
the wind and waves would not cease,
'a certain personage' took these breaking
waves as a subject, and composed this
verse :

> Never hoar-frost falls
> On the ocean stretching wide,
>   As is truly said ;
> Yet the wave-crests seem to be
> Tipped with snow far out at sea.

Ah well ! that day they had been
travelling five-and-twenty days on shipboard.[30]

22 **FEB.** 17*th day*.—The heavy clouds
cleared away, and the moonlight just
before daybreak was very beautiful.   The
boat set out, and they went on rowing.
What could the clouds overhead and the

umi no soko mo, onaji gotoku ni nan
ari-keru. Ube mo, mukashi no onoko wa,
sao wa ugatsu nami no ue no tsuki wo,
fune wa osou umi no naka no sora wo to
wa ii ken. Kiki-sashi ni kikeru nari.
Mata, aru hito no yomeru.

> Minasoko no
> Tsuki no ue yori
> Kogu fune no
> Sao ni sawaru wa
> Katsura naruran.

Kore wo kikite, aru hito no, mata
yomeru.

> Kage mireba
> Nami no soko naru
> Hisakata no
> Sora kogi wataru
> Ware zo wabishiki.

Kaku iu ma ni, yo yōyaku ake yuku
ni, kajitori-ra ' Kuroki kumo, niwaka ni

sea beneath be compared to ? He rather
fancied that when the moon is reflected
in the waves and (the sailor) plunges
his pole down, the poets of old would
have said that the vessel was attacking
the heavens themselves in mid-ocean. He
thought he had heard something of the
kind, but was not sure. 'A certain
personage' then composed this :

> As I row along,
> At the bottom of the sea
> Lies the lovely moon ;
> There 's a bush that grows on it,[31]
> Is it that my pole has hit ?

Somebody on hearing this replied : [32]

> When I see its light
> 'Neath the waves, I seem to be
> Rowing all alone
> Far across the heavenly sky,—
> Lone and desolate am I.

With these words day at last broke,
and the ship's officers [33] said, 'Black clouds

ide-kinu. Kaze mo fukinu-beshi. Mi-fune kaeshi-ten', to iite kaeru. Kono ma ni, ame furinu. Ito wabishi.

23 FEB. *Jū hachi nichi*, nao onaji tokoro ni ari. Umi ara-kereba, fune itasazu. Kono tomari tōku miredomo, chikaku miredomo, ito omoshiroshi. Ka-karedomo, kurushi kereba, nanigoto mo oboezu. Otoko dochi wa, kokoroyari ni ya aran. Kara uta nado iu-beshi. Fune mo idasade, itazura nareba, aru hito no yomeru.

> Isoburi no
> Yosuru iso ni wa
> Toshi tsuki wo
> Itsu tomo wakanu
> Yuki nomi zo furu.

have unexpectedly come up, a storm is approaching and the gallant ship must put back again.' So they returned ; just then the rain began to fall and he felt very melancholy.

23 FEB. 18*th day.*—They were still at the same spot. As long as the sea remains rough they will never get there. This stopping-place was very beautiful, whether looked at from afar or close at hand; but under the present conditions they were all too weary to take any pleasure in it. In order to pass the time, as it was hopeless to expect the boat to start, the men composed classical verses, &c., together, and ' a certain personage ' produced this :

> On this sandy shore
> Never cease the waves to break
> Year and month alike ;
> Though 'tis white as if with snow,
> When it fell I do not know.

Kono uta wa, tsune ni senu hito no koto nari. Mata, aru hito no yomeru.

> Kaze yosuru
> Nami no iso ni wa
> Uguisu mo
> Haru mo e shiranu
> Hana nomi zo saku.

Kono uta-domo wo, sukoshi yoroshi to kikite, fune no osashi keru okina, tsukigoro no kurushiki kokoroyari ni yomeru.

> Tatsu nami wo
> Yuki ka hana ka to
> Fuku kaze ni
> Yose-tsutsu hito wo
> Hakaru-bera naru.

Kono uta-domo wo, hito no nanika to iu wo, aru hito no mata kiki-fukerite yomeru. Sono uta yomeru moji, miso

This verse was like an amateur's attempt, so he tried again as follows :

Though upon the shore
Wind-blown waves break into foam
    White like flowers in bloom,
Neither nightingales nor spring
Knew these flowers were blossoming.

On hearing it said that these verses were pretty good, ' the venerable master of the ship,'[34] to distract his thoughts, which had been gloomy for a month, composed this :

Driven by the wind,
Stormy billows getting up
    Crested white with foam
Make me think them tipped with snow,
Or that 'tis the flowers that blow.

Several people criticized these verses, and one man, who was much interested in them, made another one. But, as his verse had seven-and-thirty syllables,[35]

moji amari nana moji, hito mina e arade
warau yō nari. Uta-nushi ito keshiki
ashiku emazu. Manebe-domo, e mane-
bazu. Kakeri-domo e yomi aegatakaru-
beshi. Kyō dani ii katashi. Mashite,
nochi ni wa ikanaran.

24 FEB. *Jū ku nichi*, hi ashi kereba,
fune idasazu.

25 FEB. *Hatsuka*, kinō no yō nareba,
fune idasazu. Mina, hito-bito uree nageku, kurushiku kokoro mo to nakereba,
tada hi no henuru kazu wo, kyō ikuka,
hatsuka, misoka to kazōreba, oyobi mo
sokonawarenu-beshi. Yo wa i mo nezu.
Ito wabishi. Hatsuka no yo no tsuki ide
ni keri. Yama no ha mo nakute, umi
no naka yori zo ide-kuru. Kōyō naru

the others could not help laughing.
The poet, however, kept a grave face and
did not even smile. I could not make a
verse like that if I tried ; if it was written
down, I doubt if I could read it ; and
if I find it hard now, who could ever
manage it in the future ?

24 FEB. 19*th day*.—The weather was
bad, so the boat could not start.

25 FEB. 20*th day*.—Just as yesterday the
boat could not start. All the people were
sighing most dolefully, for their hearts
were sad at wasting so many days. How
many did they amount to already? Twenty?
Thirty ? It would make my fingers ache
to count them. At night he could not
sleep and was in a melancholy mood. The
rising moon, twenty days old, came up
out of the midst of the sea, for there were
no mountain-tops (for it to rise from).
With reference to that, men say that in

wo mite ya, mukashi, Abe no Naka Maro
to ii keru hito wa, Morokoshi ni watarite,
kaeri-kuru toki ni, fune ni noru-beki
tokoro nite, kano kuni-bito, uma no
hanamukeshi, wakare oshimite, kashiko
no Kara uta tsukuri nado shi keru.
Akazu ya ari-ken. Hatsuka no yo no
tsuki izuru made zo ari-keru. Sono
tsuki wa, umi yori zo ide-keru. Kore wo
mite, Naka Maro no nushi, ' Waga Kuni
ni wa, kakaru uta wo nan, Kami-yo yori,
Kami mo yomi-tabi, ima wa kami naka
shimo no hito mo, kayō ni wakare oshimi,
yorokobi mo ari, kanashimi mo aru toki
ni wa yomu ' tote, yomeri keru uta.

> ' Ao unabara
> Furisake-mireba
>   Kasuga naru
> Mikasa no Yama ni
> Ideshi tsuki kamo.'

the old days, when Abe no Naka Maro [36] was about to cross over from China on his return, some of the country-folk at the place of his embarkation gave him a farewell banquet, to show their regret at his departure, and he then composed a classical poem. They did not grow weary until the moon rose on the night of the twentieth day; and it was from the sea that the moon rose then also. While gazing at it the great master Naka Maro (said), ' In my land in the time of the Gods the Deities themselves always composed poems like this; and still to-day all the people of the upper, middle and lower classes do the same, when bidding a sad farewell, and in times of joy and sorrow.' He then composed this :

> ' I, while gazing far
> O'er the blue sea stretching wide,
>   Seem to see the moon
> Rising o'er Mount Mikasa
> At the Shrine of Kasuga.' [37]

To zo yomeru. Kano kuni no hito, kiki-shirumajiku oboetaredomo, koto no kokoro wo, otoko moji ni sama wo kaki-idashite, koko no kotoba tsutaetaru hito ni, ii shirase kereba, kokoro wo ya kiki-eritari ken. Ito omoi no hoka ni nan medetari keru. Morokoshi to, kono kuni to wa, kotoba kotonaru mono naredo, tsuki no kage wa onaji koto narube kereba, hito no kokoro mo onaji koto ni ya aran. Sate ima sonokami wo omoiyarite, aru hito no yomeru uta.

Miyako nite
Yama no ha ni mishi
Tsuki naredo
Nami yori idete
Nami ni koso ire.

26 FEB. *Nijū ichi nichi*, U no Toki bakari ni funadesu. Mina, hito-bito no fune izu. Kore wo mireba, haru no umi

That is the verse.   Though the people of that land did not seem to understand it when they heard it, yet when the proper words were written down in men's characters (Chinese ideographs) they understood it perfectly, and were much pleased with it.[38]   In that far away land of China the language was different, but the moonlight was still the same, and would not the hearts of men be the same also ?   With his thoughts still fixed upon those days, ' a certain personage ' composed this verse :

> In the Capital
> Oft I saw the moon arise
>   O'er the mountain-tops ;
> Now she rises from the main
> Sinking in the waves again.

26 FEB. 21*st day*.—The boat set forth about the Hour of the Hare (6.0 a.m.). Many other boats started as well, and the sight seemed to him like autumn leaves scattered upon the sea, although it was

ni aki no ko no ha shimo, chireru yō ni zo ari-keru. Oboroge no negai ni yorite ni ya aran. Kaze mo fukazu, yoki hi ide kite, kogi yuku. Kono ma ni, tsukawaren tote tsuki-kuru warawa ari. Sore ga utau funa-uta, ' Nao koso kuni no kata wa miyararure, waga chichi haha ari to shi omoeba, kaeraya,' to utau zo aware naru. Kaku utau wo kiki-tsutsu kogi kuru ni, kurotori to iu tori, iwao no ue ni atsumari ori, sono iwao no moto ni, nami shiroku uchi yosu, kajitori no iu yō, ' Kurotori no moto ni, shiroki nami wo yosu' to zo iu. Kono kotoba, nani to ni wa nakeredo, mono iu yō ni zo kikoetaru. Hito no hodo ni awaneba, togamuru nari. Kaku ii-tsutsu yuku ni, funagimi naru hito, nami wo mite, Kuni yori hajimete, kaizoku mukui sen to iu

spring time. There was no breath of
wind—no doubt in answer to their
prayers for haze—and the sun was shining
brightly as they set out rowing. About
this time a boy who had come as his
servant sang this boat song, ' Still can I
cast my gaze far o'er the country-side ;
when I think of my father and of my
mother, I long to return to them again.'[39]
It was quite pathetic to hear him singing
this, and the boat rowed on while they
were still listening to it. Some birds called
blackbirds were clustered upon the cliffs,
and at the foot of these cliffs the waves
were breaking into foam. The steersman
remarked, ' Under the blackbirds the
white waves are breaking ! ' These words,
whatever they might be worth, sounded
remarkable, and, as he had never met a
man like that before, he was much struck
with them. At these words and while still
travelling on, he who was ' the passenger '
noticed the waves, and remembered

naru koto wo omou ue ni, umi no mata osoroshi kereba, kashira mo mina shira-kenu. Shichi jū hachi jū wa, umi ni arumono nari-keri.

> Waga kami no
> Yuki to isobe no
> Shira nami to
> Izure masareri
> Okitsu-shima Mori.

Kajitori ie.

27 **FEB.** *Nijū ni nichi*, yobe no tomari yori, koto-tomari wo oite yuku. Haruka ni yama miyu. Toshi kokonotsu bakari naru o no warawa, toshi yori wa osanaku zo aru. Kono warawa, fune wo kogu mani-mani, yama mo yuku to miyuru wo mite, ayashiki uta wo zo yomeru. Sono uta,

> Kogite yuku
> Fune nite mireba

that the pirates had threatened to take
revenge upon him, when once he had
left the Province; all his hair turned
white, when the waves once more became
rough. Seventy or eighty years are what
one must expect at sea ![40]

> White as snow my hair,
> Waves roll in upon the shore
>   Breaking into foam ;
> Which is whiter ? Can'st thou say,
> Warder of the Isles, I pray ?

Tell me, steersman.

27 FEB. *22nd day*.—They rowed on
from last night's stopping-place to the next
one. In the distance the hills were
visible, and a lad on board, who was but
nine years old and looked much younger,
fancied that these hills seemed to be following the boat as it was being rowed along,
and composed this quaint verse :

> While I watch the shore
> From the swiftly moving ship,

> Ashibiki no
> Yama sae yuku wo
> Matsu wa shirazu ya.

To zo ieru. Osanaki warawa no koto nite wa, nitsukawashi. Kyō umi arake, iso ni yuki furi, nami no hana sakeri. Aru hito no yomeru.

> Nami to nomi
> Hitoe ni kikedo
> Iro mireba
> Yuki to hana to ni
> Magainuru kana.

28 FEB. *Nijū san nichi*, hi terite kumorinu. Kono watari, kaizoku no osori ari to ieba, Kami Hotoke wo inoru.

1 MAR. *Nijū yokka*, kinō no onaji tokoro nari.

Do the pine trees guess,
That the hills on which they grow
Seem to move along also ?

So he sang. How characteristic it is
of a young lad's fancy ! This day the
sea was rough, and the waves broke into
blossom, falling like snow upon the beach ;
whereupon ' a certain personage ' composed this :

Not a sound I hear,
Save the tumult of the waves
Breaking into foam.
Much I wonder at the sight,—
Mingled snow and blossoms white !

28 FEB. *23rd day*.—The sun shone
forth from the clouds, and, as there was
said to be danger of pirates during the
voyage, he prayed for protection to the
Shintō and Buddhist Gods.

1 MAR. *24th day*.—They remained at
the same place as the day before.

2 MAR. *Nijū go nichi*, kajitori-ra no, kita kaze ashi to ieba, fune idasazu. Kaizoku oiku to iu koto, taezu kikoyu.

3 MAR. *Nijū roku nichi*, makoto ni ya aran. Kaizoku ou to ieba, yowa bakari yori fune wo idashite, kogi kuru michi ni, tamuke suru tokoro ari. Kajitori shite, nusa tatematsura suru ni, nusa no hingashi e chireba, kajitori no mōshite tatematsuru koto wa, ' Kono nusa no chiru kata ni, mi-fune sumiyaka ni kogashime tamae ' to mōshite, tatematsuru. Kore wo kikite, aru warawa no yomeru.

> Watatsumi no
> Chiburi no Kami ni
> Tamuke suru
> Nusa no oi kaze
> Yamazu fukanan.

2 MAR. 25*th* *day*.—The ship's officers said the north wind was unfavourable, so the boat did not start. There were many reports going about that the pirates were actually in pursuit !

3 MAR. 26*th* *day*.—Can this really be true ? As they say the pirates are in chase, the boat is not to start before mid-night, and offerings are to be made while rowing. The steersman accordingly offered prayer-papers,[41] and, as these fluttered away to the east, he prayed, ' Graciously allow our gallant ship to be rowed with all speed in the direction taken by these prayer-papers.' On hearing this a child made the following verse :

> To the Deep Sea God,
> He who rules the ocean road,
>   Make we now our prayer ;
> For these flying *nusa*, pray,
> May the breeze not die away.

To zo yomeru. Kono ma ni, kaze yo-kereba, kajitori itaku hokorite, fune ni ho age yorokobu. Sono oto wo kikite, warawa mo, onna mo, itsushika to shi omoeba ni ya aran. Itaku yorokobu. Kono uchi ni, Awaji no Tōme to iu hito no yomeru uta,

> Oi kaze no
> Fukinuru toki wa
> Yuku fune no
> Hote uchite koso
> Ureshi-kari kere.

To zo. Teike no koto ni tsuke-tsutsu inoru.

4 MAR. *Nijū shichi nichi,* kaze fuki nami ara-kereba, fune idasazu. Kore-kare kashikoku nageku, otoko-tachi no ko-koro nagusame ni, Kara uta ni, hi wo

This was her verse. As the wind was
fair at the moment, the steersman was
proud and happy in hoisting sail on the
boat ; and the women and children, as
they heard the sound, were delighted,
for they thought that now (they would
surely arrive) sooner or later. Among them
all one called the Matron of Awaji [42]
composed this :

> When the kindly breeze
> Follows up behind the boat,
>   Fast we speed along ;
> As we hoist the sail with glee, [43]
> Happy and content are we.

And at the same time she prayed for
fine weather.

4 MAR. 27th day.—The wind blew,
the waves were rough, and the boat could
not start. They were all complaining
dreadfully ; so the men, to cheer up their
hearts, composed a Chinese poem, to the

nozomeba Miyako tōshi nado iu naru
koto no sama wo kikite, aru onna no
yomeru uta,

> Hi wo dani mo
> Ama-gumo chikaku
> Miru mono wo
> Miyako e to omou
> Michi no harukesa.

Mata, aru hito no yomeru.

> Fuku kaze no
> Taenu kagirishi
> Tachi-kureba
> Nami-ji wa itodo
> Haruke-kari keri.

Hi hito hi, kaze yamazu. Tsuma
hajiki wo shite nenu.

5 **MAR.** *Nijū hachi nichi*, yomosugara
ame yamazu. Kesa mo.

effect that the Capital was further away than the sun itself ; and on hearing it a certain woman composed this :

> In the sky the clouds
> Ever nearer seem to draw,
>   E'en the sun as well ;
> But the Capital to-day
> Still seems very far away.

To this ' a certain personage ' replied :

> Loud the tempests roar,
> Not an instant dying down
>   As we travel on,
> And our road across the sea
> Ever longer seems to be.[44]

All day long the wind did not drop ; so he snapped his fingers [45] and retired to rest.

5 MAR. 28th day.—The rain did not stop all through the night, nor in the morning either.

6 MAR. *Nijū ku nichi*, fune idashite yuku, ura-ura to terite kogi yuku, tsume no ito nagaku nari nitaru wo mite, hi wo kazōreba, kyō wa Ne no Hi nari kereba, kirazu. Mutsuki nareba, Miyako no Ne no Hi no koto ii idete, komatsu mogana to iedo, umi naka nareba, katashi kashi. Aru onna no kakite, idaseru uta,

> Obotsukana
> Kyō wa Ne no Hi ka
> Ama naraba
> Umi-matsu wo dani
> Hikamashi mono wo.

To zo ieru. Umi nite, Ne no Hi no uta nite wa, ikaga aran. Mata, aru hito no yomeru uta,

> Kyō naredo
> Wakana mo tsumazu

6 MAR. *29th day.*—The boat set out
and the sun shone brightly as they went
on rowing. Noticing that his nails had
grown very long, he counted the days
and found that it was a ' Day of the
Rat ' [46]—they must not be cut. As it
was the first month, they chatted about
the Day of the Rat in the Capital, and
wished there were some young pine trees
(for them to pull up) ; but, as they were
out at sea, such things were hard to find.
A certain woman wrote this verse :

Is it really true
That to-day is *Ne no Hi* ?
Were I a fish-wife,
I would dive down through the brine
And pull up the salt sea-pine.[47]

Those were her words ; but how can
one write a Day of the Rat verse at sea ?
' A certain personage ' replied with this :

Though this is the day,
Yet we cannot pick the greens

Kasuga No no
Waga kogi wataru
Ura ni nakereba.

Kaku ii-tsutsu, kogi yuku. Omo-
shiroki tokoro ni, fune wo yosete, koko ya
izuko to toi-kereba, 'Tosa no Tomari' to
zo ii-keru. Mukashi, Tosa to ii-keru
tokoro ni sumi keru onna, kono fune ni
majiri keri. Sore ga ii-keraku, mukashi,
shibashi arishi tokoro no na tagui ni zo
anaru. Aware to iite, yomeru uta,

Toshigoro wo
Sumishi tokoro no
Na nishi oeba
Ki-yoru nami wo mo
Aware to zo miru.

7 **MAR.** *Misoka*, ame kaze fukazu.
Kaizoku wa, yo ariki seza nari to kikite,

On Kasuga Moor ;
Never were they known to grow
On the shore, past which we row.

They went on rowing, while he was
reciting this. On the boat approaching
a delightful spot, he asked what place it
was, and was told it was called ' Tosa
Stopping-Place '. There was a woman on
board,[48] who had once lived in the land
called Tosa, and she said that in past days
she had known a place of that name,
but only for a short time. To express
her regret for it, she composed this
verse :

Musing on the name
Of the place where once I lived
For a year or so,—
Billows rolling in from sea
Come to sympathize with me.

7 MAR. 30th day.—The wind and rain
had stopped ; and so, hearing that the

yo-naka bakari, fune wo idashite, Awa no Mito wo wataru. Yo-naka nareba, nishi himugashi wo miezu. Otoko onna, karaku Kami Hotoke wo inorite, kono mito wo watarinu. Tora U no Toki bakari ni, Nujima to iu tokoro wo sugite, Tanagawa to iu tokoro wo wataru. Karaku isogite, Izumi no Nada to iu tokoro ni itarinu. Kyō, umi ni nami ni nitaru mono nashi Kami Hotoke no megumi kōbureru ni nitari. Kyō fune ni norishi hi yori kazōreba, misoka amari kokonoka ni nari ni keri. Ima wa, Izumi no Kuni ni kinureba, kaizoku mono narazu.

8 MAR. *Ni gwatsu tsuitachi*, asa no ma ame furi, Uma no Toki bakari ni

pirates never travel by night, the boat set
out to cross the Awa Channel at midnight.
It was so dark that they could not see
which was east and which was west ; but
men and women prayed earnestly to the
Shintō and Buddhist Gods, and so the
dreaded channel was crossed in safety.   It
was not till the Hour of the Tiger or the
Hare (4.0 or 6.0 a.m.) that they passed the
Isle of Nujima, crossed (the mouth of)
the Tanagawa, and, hurrying on as fast
as possible, reached the Sea of Izumi.
That day there were no waves upon the
sea, thanks to the blessings vouchsafed
by the Shintō and Buddhist Gods.   Up
to date the days passed on board ship
amounted to nine-and-thirty days.   Now
that they had reached the Land of Izumi,
there was no further question of pirates.

8 MAR. 1st day of the 2nd month.—Rain
fell in the morning, and stopped only at
the Hour of the Horse (noon).   Passing

yaminureba, Izumi no Nada to iu tokoro yori idete, kogi yuku. Umi no ue, kinō no gotoku ni, kaze nami miezu. Kuro Saki no matsubara wo hete-yuku, tokoro no na wa kuroku, matsu no iro wa aoku. Iso no nami wa yuki no gotoku ni shiroku, kai no iro wa suō nite, go shiki ni, ima hito iro zo taranu. Kono ma ni, kyō wa Hako no Ura to iu tokoro yori, tsunade wo hikite yuku, kaku yuku aida ni aru hito no yomeru uta,

Tamakushige
Hako no Ura nami
Tatanu hi wa
Umi wo kagami to
Tare ka mizaran.

Mata, funagimi no iwaku. Kono tsuki made narinuru koto tote nagekite,

through the Sea of Izumi, they rowed on.
Just as yesterday no wind-tossed waves
were visible at sea. They passed the pine
forest on Black Head. The name of the
headland was black, the colour of its pines
green, the breakers upon the shore white
as snow, and the tint of its shells pink;
so that only one colour was wanting to
complete the five primary colours.[49] That
day the boat was towed by a rope from the
place named Casket Beach, and while
travelling thus ' a certain personage '
composed this :

> Not a ripple breaks
> On the shore at Casket Beach,
> Fair as jewel box;[50]
> Could the brightest looking-glass
> Such a sea as this surpass?

Once again ' the passenger ' spoke,
lamenting that (the voyage) had lasted
into this month, and for the many
hardships they had endured, to which the

kurushiki ni taezu shite, hito mo iu koto
tote, kokoro yari ni ieru uta.

> Hiku fune no
> Tsunade no nagaki
> Haru no hi wo
> Yosoka ika made
> Ware wa he ni keri.

Kiku hito no omoeru yō, nazo tada
goto naru to, hisoka ni iu-beshi. Funagimi no karaku hineri idashite, yoshi to
omoru koto wo, e shi mo koso shii-ne
tote, sasamekite yaminu. Niwaka ni,
kaze nami taka kereba, todomarinu.

9 MAR. *Futsuka,* ame kaze yamazu.
Hi hito hi, yomosugara, Kami Hotoke wo
inoru.

10 MAR. *Mikka,* umi no ue, kinō no
yō nareba, fune idasazu, kaze no fuku

others agreed. Out of the fullness of his heart he recited this :

> Though the days in spring
> Grow as long as is the rope
> Used to tow our boat,
> Forty days we've spent,—maybe
> Fifty days upon the sea.

People who hear this will say to themselves that this kind of stuff is very poor. But ' the passenger ' produced it with a good deal of difficulty and thought it pretty good ; so they should stop whispering such cruel things about it. But suddenly the wind and waves got up, and so they had to stop talking.

9 MAR. *2nd day.*—The wind and rain did not cease. For a whole day and night they prayed to the Shintō and Buddhist Gods.

10 MAR. *3rd day.*—Out at sea it was just like yesterday, so the boat did not

koto yamaneba, kishi no nami tachi-kaeru.
Kore ni tsukete yomeru uta.

> O wo yorite
> Kainaki mono wa
> Ochi tsumoru
> Namida no tama wo
> Nukanu nari keri.

Kakute, kyō mo kurenu.

11 **MAR.** *Yokka*, kajitori, kyō kaze
kumo no keshiki hanahada ashi to iite,
fune idasazu narinu. Shikaredomo, hinemosu ni, nami kaze tatazu. Kono kajitori
wa, hi mo e hakaranu katai nari keri.
Kono tomari no hama ni wa, kusagusa no
uruwashiki kai, ishi nado ōkari. Kakareba,

start.   The howling gale did not abate, and the waves dashed up against the cliffs and drew back again.   Noting this, he composed the following :

Fast my teardrops fall,
But to twist a silken thread
    Surely would be vain ;
Who could thread up pearls so frail?
All my skill would not avail.[51]

And thus the day drew to its close.

11 MAR. 4*th day*.—The steersman said that the wind-blown clouds looked very threatening to-day, so the boat did not set out.   However, the wind and waves did not get up the whole day long ; this steersman was not always right in his forecasts of the weather.   Beautiful shells of many kinds and pebbles were plentiful on the shore where they camped ; and with reference to them somebody

tada, mukashi no hito wo nomi koi-tsutsu,
fune naru hito no yomeru,

> Yosuru nami
> Uchi mo yosenan
> Waga kōru
> Hito wasure-gai
> Orite hirowan.

To iereba, aru hito no taezu shite, fune
no kokoro yari ni yomeru.

> Wasure-gai
> Hiroi shi mo seji
> Shira tama wo
> Kōru wo dani mo
> Katami to omowan.

To nan ieru. Onna no ko no tame ni
wa, oya osanaku narinu-beshi. Tama
narazu mo ari ken wo to, hito iwan ya.
Saredomo, shinishi ko, kao yokariki to
iu yō mo ari. Nao onaji tokoro ni hi wo

belonging to the ship composed this verse
in memory of one who was much loved :

> Here the breaking waves
> Come and go, as I lament
> For my darling child ;
> Stooping I, to bid farewell,
> Pick up a ' forgetting-shell '.[52]

Such were her words ; but ' a certain
personage ', unable to bear it any longer,
composed this, to give heart to the others
in the ship :

> Here no more we'll stray
> Seeking for ' forgetting-shells ' ;
> But a dainty pearl
> Pure and white might serve to tell
> Of the child we loved so well.

Thus he spoke in memory of his little
daughter, for a parent is apt to become
very childish.   Some may object that she
was not like a pearl ; be that as it may,
the child is dead, and it is no empty

furu koto wo nagekite, aru onna no
yomeru uta.

> Te wo hidete
> Samusa mo shiranu
> Izumi ni zo
> Kumu to wa nashi ni
> Higoro he ni keru.

12 MAR. *Itsuka*, kyō karaku shite,
Izumi no Nada yori, Ozu no Tomari
wo ou. Matsubara me mo harubaru nari,
karekore kurushi kereba yomeru uta,

> Yukedo nao
> Yuki yararenu wa
> Imo ga umu
> Ozu no ura naru
> Kishi no matsubara.

Kaku ii-tsutsu kuru hodo ni, fune toku

compliment to say she had a beautiful
face. A certain woman composed this
verse in grief at the number of days
spent in the same place :

> Long we've soaked our hands
> In Izumi's icy spring
> Dreading not the cold ;
> Here though many days we waste,
> 'Tis a spring we never taste.[53]

12 MAR. 5*th* *day.*—This day with
difficulty they hastened on through the
Sea of Izumi to the Stopping-Place of
Ozu. To his eye the pine forests seemed
never-ending, everything seemed to have
gone wrong, and he composed this :

> Though we speed along,
> Yet the pine trees on the cliffs
> Never seem to pass ;
> Long as thread is Ozu strand
> Spun out by a maiden's hand.[54]

At these words and while they still
travelled on, the steersman called to the

koge, hi no yoki ni to moyōseba, kajitori
funago-domo ni iwaku, 'Mi-fune yori
ōse-tabu nari asagita no, ide konu saki
ni, tsunade haya hike' to iu. Kono
kotoba no uta no yō naru wa, kajitori
no onozukara no kotoba nari. Kajitori
wa, uttae ni, ware uta no yō naru koto
iu to ni mo arazu. Kiku hito no ayashiku uta-mekite mo ieru kana tote, kaki
idasereba, geni miso moji amari nari
keri. Kyō, nami na tachi soto, hito-bito
hinemosu ni inoru shirushi arite, kaze
nami tatazu, imashi, kamome mure ite,
asobu tokoro ari. Miyako no chikazuku
yorokobi no amari ni, aru warawa no
yomeru uta.

Inori kuru
Kaza-ma to omou wo

sailors to pull hard, for the weather was about to improve. ' On this gallant ship my command must be obeyed ; this is what I say,—ere the morning north wind blow, get the rope ashore and tow,' said he. The poetic form of these words was quite unintentional on the part of the steersman ; and, on being appealed to, he said he did not mean it for a verse ; but, on putting into writing the queer poetical sentence the man was heard to say, there proved indeed to be just over thirty syllables (i.e. thirty-one syllables).[55] This day every one prayed all day long that the waves outside might not arise ; and in answer to their prayers the wind and waves did not get up. Soon (they arrived at) a place where flocks of seagulls sported about, and, in an excess of joy at getting so near the Capital, a child composed this :

Though the wind has dropped,
For the Gods have heard our prayers,

Ayanaku mo
Kamome sae dani
Nami to miyuran.

To iite, yuku ma ni, Iwatsu to iu tokoro no matsubara, omoshirokute, hamabe tōshi. Mata, Sumiyoshi no watari wo kogi yuku. Aru hito no yomeru.

Ima mite zo
Mi woba shirinuru
Suminoye no
Matsu yori saki ni
Ware wa he ni keri.

Koko ni, mukashi tsu hito no haha, hito hi, kata-toki mo wasureneba,

Suminoye no
Fune sashi-yose-yo
Wasure-gusa
Shirushi ari ya to
Tsumite yuku-beku.

In my dizzy brain
Swooping seagulls look to me
Like the ever surging sea.

While she recited this, they travelled on. The pine forest at a place called Iwatsu was very beautiful, but the shore seemed interminable. Once more, as they rowed past Sumiyoshi, 'a certain personage' composed this :

Suminoye's pines,[56]
As I watch them, seem to be
Younger far than I ;
I shall vanish from the scene,
But the pines are evergreen.

And here the mother of one now gone, whom she never forgets for a day, or even for a moment :

Urge the boat along,
On to Suminoye beach,
For I long to pick
Some 'forgetting-grass', [57] to see
If it will come true with me.

To nan, uttae ni wasurenan to ni wa arade, koishiki kokochi, shibashi yasumete, mata mo kōru chikara ni sen to naru-beshi. Kaku iite, nagame-tsutsu kuru ma ni, yukurinaku kaze fuki ide, koge-domo koge-domo shirie ni shizoki ni shizokite, hodo-hodo shiku, uchi-hametsu-beshi. Kajitori no iwaku. 'Kono Sumiyoshi no Myōjin wa, tameshi no Kami zo kashi. Hoshiki mono zo owasuran' to wa, imameku mono ka. Sate nusa wo tai-matsuri-tamae to iu ni shitagaite, nusa taimatsuru. Kaku tatematsure-domo, mohara, kaze ya made, iya fuki ni, iya tachi ni, kaze nami no ayau-kereba, kajitori mata iwaku. 'Nusa ni wa, mi-kokoro no yuru-kaneba, mi-fune mo yu-kanu nari. Nao, ureshi to omoi tamau-beki mono tatematsuri-tamae' to iu.

This she said, not because she wished to forget really, but she hoped that her sorrow might find some short relief, in order that her love might return stronger than ever. With these words then they travelled on, while still gazing at the prospect. But suddenly the wind arose; and, though they rowed hard, they drifted quickly astern and nearly capsized, when they must all have been lost. The steersman said, ' This holy Deity of Sumiyoshi is a well-known God, and he desires some gift.' How like everybody else ! Some one suggested that *nusa* should be offered; so accordingly an offering of prayer-papers was made. But, though it was done chiefly for the wind to abate, it began to blow harder than ever and the waves rose accordingly, so that they were in great danger. Then the steersman spoke again, and said, ' As the august heart (of the God) has not been moved by the prayer-papers, the gallant

Mata iu ni shitagaite, ikaga wa sen tote, manako mo koso futatsu are, tada hitotsu aru kagami wo tatematsuru tote, umi ni uchi hametsureba, ito kuchi-oshi. Sareba, uchitsuke ni, umi wa kagami no goto narinureba, aru hito no yomeru uta,

Chi-haya-buru
Kami no kokoro wo
Aruru umi ni
Kagami wo irete
Katsu mitsuru kana.

Itaku, Suminoye no wasure-gusa, kishi no hime-matsu nado iu Kami ni wa arazu kashi. Me mo utsura-utsura, kagami ni, Kami no mi-kokoro wo koso wa mitsure. Kajitori no kokoro wa, Kami no mi-kokoro nari keri.

ship cannot proceed; in making an offering, therefore, something should be presented that will be thought of value.' Accordingly, what was to be done ! He had two eyes, but could offer only one mirror [58] ; so to his deep regret it was thrown into the sea. Well, immediately the sea became as calm as the looking-glass itself ! and 'a certain personage' composed this :

> In the raging sea
> I have cast my looking-glass,
>   And the gift's result
> Shows the partiality
> Of the awful Deity.

Verily there are no Gods as kindly as the 'forgetting-grass' of Suminoye or the delicate pines upon its cliffs. Plainly in the mirror could his eyes see the august heart of the God—which was remarkably like the heart of the steersman ! [59]

13 **MAR.** *Muika*, Miotsukushi no moto
yori idete, Naniwa no tsu okite, kawa-
shiri ni iru. Mina, hito-bito, onna,
osanaki mono, hitai ni te wo atete yorokobu koto, futatsu nashi. Kano funa-ei
no Awaji no Shima no Ōiko, Miyako
chikaku narinu to iu wo yorokobite,
funa-zoko yori, kashira wo motagete,
kaku zo ieru.

Itsushika to
Ibusekari-tsuru
Naniwa gata
Ashi kogi sokete
Mi-fune ki ni keri.

Ito omoi no hoka naru hito no iereba,
hito-bito ayashigaru. Kore ga naka ni,
kokochi nayamu funagimi, itaku medete,
funa-ei shitamaishi mi-kao ni wa, nizu
mo aru kana to ii keru.

13 MAR. *6th day.*—They left Miotsukushi,[60] reached the port of Naniwa and
entered the mouth of the river. Every one,
men, women, and children, lifted their
hands to their foreheads and exclaimed
in delight, 'There is nothing like this!'
The Old Lady of Awaji Isle was sea-sick;
but on hearing that they were getting near
the Capital, she raised her head from the
bottom of the boat and in her delight
recited this verse:

> Many doubts had I
> On the day we first set forth;
> Now our gallant ship
> Gently glides, from danger far,
> 'Mid the reeds of Naniwa.

Everybody was astonished when she
came out with this so unexpectedly; and
among them 'the passenger', who was
also feeling unwell, praised it very highly,
and said it was not what he had expected
from one with such a sea-sick countenance.

14 MAR. *Nanuka*, kyō kawa-shiri ni fune iri-tachite, kogi noboru ni, kawa no mizu hite nayami wazurau. Fune no noboru koto, ito katashi. Kakaru ma ni, funagimi no yama-udo, moto yori kochigochi shiki hito nite, kōyō no koto, sara ni shirazari keri. Kakare-domo, Awaji no Tōme no uta ni medete, Miyako bokori ni mo ya aran. Karakushite, ayashiki uta hito tsu hineri idaseri. Sono uta,

> Kito kite wa
> Kawa no hori e no
> Mizu wo asami
> Fune mo waga mi mo
> Nazumu kyō kana.

Kore wa, yamai wo sureba, yomeru naru-beshi. Hito uta ni, koto no akaneba, ima hitotsu,

> Toku to omou
> Fune nayamasu wa

14 MAR. *7th day.*—This day the boat left the mouth of the river; but as they rowed on, the river tide was ebbing, and they were in great difficulty. To get the boat up was very hard. At this ' the sick passenger ', who was not very practical by nature, was wholly at a loss to know what should be done. However, he was so pleased with the Matron of Awaji's verse, that he comforted himself with the thought that he would soon be at the Capital; and so with some difficulty he turned out this very doubtful verse:

> Here at last are we,
> But how shallow runs the stream
>   In the river bed;
> Further can the boat not go,
> Here must we remain also.

It was because he was so unwell that he composed this poor sort of thing. As he was not satisfied with it, here is another:

> Fast we'd hurry on,
> If the river's shallow bed

Waga tame ni
Mizu no kokoro no
Asaki nari keri.

Kono uta wa, Miyako chikaku narinuru
yorokobi ni taezu shite, ieru naru-beshi.
Awaji no Go no uta ni otoreri. Netaku,
iwazaramashi mono wo to, kuyashigaru
uchi ni, yo ni narite ne ni keri.

15 MAR. *Yōka*, nao kawa no hotori
ni nazumite, 'Torikai no Mimaki' to iu
hotori ni todomaru. Koyoi, funagimi, rei
no yamai okorite, itaku nayamu. Aru
hito, isasaka naru mono mote kitari, yone
shite kaeri-goto su. Otoko-domo, hisoka ni
iu nari. 'Iibo shite mo tsuru' to ya. Kōyō
no koto, tokoro-dokoro ni ari. Kyō sechimi sureba, uo mochi-izu.

Did not stay our boat.
As the stream runs dry, maybe
It has got a grudge at me.

These verses should be understood as composed when he could not repress his joy at getting so near the Capital; but they are not as good as the one by her Ladyship of Awaji, and feeling jealous of her he regretted having made them ; so, as the night was drawing on, he retired to sleep.

15 **MAR.** 8*th day*.—Still keeping to the river-side, they stopped at a place called 'The Gamekeeper's Preserve'. That evening 'the passenger' suffered severely from his chronic complaint.[61] There was a man who came with some trifling gift, who got some rice in return (i.e. a large present) ; and the men whispered among themselves, that he had come 'to fish with a grain of rice'. But this sort of thing may happen anywhere. This day he was fasting and ate no fish.

16 MAR. *Kokonoka*, kokoromotonaki ni akenu kara, fune wo hiki-tsutsu nobore-domo, kawa no mizu nakereba, izari ni nomi zo izaru. Kono ma ni, Wada no Tomari no, 'Agare no Tokoro' to iu tokoro ari. Kome, uwo nado koyeba, okosetsu. Kakute, fune hiki noboru ni, 'Nagisa no In' to iu tokoro wo mi-tsutsu yuku. Sono In, mukashi wo omoi-yarite mireba, omoshirokari keru tokoro nari. Shirie naru oka ni wa, matsu no ki-domo ari. Mae no niwa ni wa, ume no hana sakeri. Koto ni, hito-bito no iwaku. Kore wa mukashi nadakaku kikoetaru tokoro nari. Koretaka no Miko no On tomo ni, Ariwara no Narihira no Chūjō no,

'Yo no naka ni
Taete sakura no

16 MAR. *9th day*.—From early dawn he was very anxious. They ascended the river towing the boat; but, as there was hardly any water in the river, they had to push and haul it along. At last they came to a place called 'The Parting of the Ways' at the Stopping-Place of Wada, and there rice and fish were supplied to them at their request. While towing the boat up like this, they saw on their way a place called 'The Shore Residence'. This Residence, as one pictured to oneself the days of old, was a very delightful spot. On the hill behind were many pine trees, while in the garden in front the plum trees were in full blossom. Here, they said, here was a place famous in past days; for on this spot General Ariwara no Narihira lived in companionship with His Royal Highness Prince Koretaka.

'If the cherry trees
Nevermore burst forth in bloom,

Sakazaraba
Haru no kokoro wa
Nodokekara-mashi.'

To iu uta yomeru tokoro nari keri.
Ima, kyō aru hito, tokoro ni nitaru uta
yomeri,

Chi yo hetaru
Matsu ni wa aredo
Inishie no
Koye no samusa wa
Kawarazari keri.

Mata, aru hito no yomeru,

Kimi koite
Yo wo furu yado no
Ume no hana
Mukashi no ka ni zo
Nao nioi keru.

To ii-tsutsu zo, Miyako no chikazuku wo yorokobi-tsutsu noboru. Kaku

'Twould be better far ;
For the saddest time of all
Is the spring, when petals fall.' [62]

And this is the spot where he composed
this verse.   Now ' a certain personage '
in his delight at the place composed
this :

For a thousand years
Have these pine trees lived, their tops
    Rustle as of old ;
'Tis a language drear and strange,
And their voice will never change.

This, also, he composed :

Still the plum trees bloom
Round this dwelling as of old,
    And in memory
Of their Lord they loved so well
Still retain their ancient smell. [63]

While these were being recited, they
went on rejoicing at getting nearer to the

noboru hito-bito no naka ni, Miyako yori
kudarishi toki ni, mina hito, ko-domo
nakariki. Itarerishi Kuni nite zo ko
umeru mono-domo ari aeru. Mina
hito, fune no tomaru tokoro ni ko wo
idaki-tsutsu, ori-noborisu. Kore wo
mite, mukashi no ko no haha kanashimi
ni taezu shite.

Nakarishi mo
Ari-tsutsu kaeru
Hito no ko wo
Arishi mo nakute
Kuru ga kanashisa.

To iite zo naki keru. Chichi mo, kore
wo kikite, ikaga aran. Kōyō no koto, uta
konomu tote, aru nishi mo arazaru-beshi.
Morokoshi mo koko mo, omou koto ni
taenu toki no waza to ka. Koyoi, Udono
to iu tokoro ni tomaru.

Capital. Among all the people thus going up, not one had any children when they left the Capital; but some had babies born in the Province. Everybody crowded down to the place where the boat stopped to embrace these children, and at the sight of this the mother of that child who is gone could no longer restrain her grief:

> Many who set forth
> Childless from the Capital
> Bring a baby back;
> One who then a daughter had
> Now returns bereft and sad.

With these words she wept. And when ' the father ' heard it, what could he do? He wished to make a similar verse, but there was no other subject. For here, as in China, (we compose a poem) when our hearts are too full of feeling. That evening they stopped at a place called Udono.

17 MAR. *Tōka*, sawaru koto arite noborazu.

18 MAR. *Jū ichi nichi*, ame isasaka furite yaminu. Kakute, sashi noboru ni, higashi no kata ni, yama no yoko-oreru wo mite, hito ni toeba, Hachiman ▗ Miya to iu. Kore wo kikite, hito-bito ogami tatematsuru. Yamasaki no Hashi miyu. Ureshiki koto kagiri nashi. Koko ni, Sōō Ji no hotori ni, shibashi fune wo todomete, tokaku satamuru koto ari. Kono tera no kishi no hotori ni, yanagi ōku ari. Aru hito, kono yanagi no kawa no soko ni utsureru wo mite, yomeru uta,

Sazare nami
Yosuru aya woba

17 MAR. 10*th day*.—There was something wrong and they did not go forward.

18 MAR. 11*th day*.—Gentle rain was falling, so they remained where they were for a little. Then, on going forward, (something) came into view to the east across the mountains, which a man on being asked said was the Temple of Hachiman.[64] On hearing this they all reverently made obeisance and offered prayers. See! there is Yamasaki Bridge! There was no limit to their delight; and there, opposite the Sōō Temple, the boat stopped for a little time, while they made their various arrangements. Near the precincts of this temple were many willow trees, and 'a certain personage' seeing them reflected at the bottom of the river composed this:

Looking o'er the stream,
Imaged on the rippling waves

Ao-yagi no
Kage no ito shite
Oru kato zo miru.

19 MAR. *Jū ni nichi*, Yamasaki ni tomareri.

20 MAR. *Jū san nichi*, nao, Yamasaki ni.

21 MAR. *Jū yokka*, ame furu. Kyō, kuruma Miyako e tori ni yaru.

22 MAR. *Jū go nichi*, kyō, kuruma ite kitari. Fune no mutsukashisa ni, fune yori hito no ie ni utsuru. Kono hito no ie yorokoberu yō nite, aruji shitari. Kono aruji no, mata, aruji no yoki wo miru ni, utate omōyu. Iro-iro ni kaeri gotosu. Ie no hito no ide iri, nikuge narazu, iyayaka nari.

As they come and go,
Hanging willow branches green
Woven like silk threads are seen.

19 MAR. 12*th day*.—They remained at
Yamasaki.

20 MAR. 13*th day*.—Still at Yamasaki.

21 MAR. 14*th day*.—Rain fell. This
day he sent to the Capital for a carriage.[65]

22 MAR. 15*th day*.—This day the
carriage arrived. Owing to the dirt on
board he removed from the boat to the
house of a friend. This friend's house
seemed indeed a delightful change, and
its owner treated him with the greatest
kindness ; so much so that he felt quite
sorry for troubling him, and tried to
make returns in many ways. Those who
entered and left the house, too, were
by no means disagreeable people, but
cultivated gentlefolk.

23 MAR. *Jū roku nichi*, kyō no yū tsu
kata, Miyako e noboru tsuide ni mireba,
Yamasaki no tana naru, ko-bitsu no
e mo, magari no hora no kata mo
kawarazari keri.   Uru hito no kokoro
wo zo shiranu to zo iu naru.   Kakute,
Miyako e iku ni, Shimasaka nite, hito
aruji shitari.   Kanarazu-shimo aru majiki
waza nari, tachite yukishi toki yori, kuru
toki zo.   Hito wa tokaku ari keru.   Kore
ni mo, sore ni mo, kaeri gotosu.   Yoru
ni nashite, Miyako ni wa iran to omoeba,
isogishi mo senu hodo ni, tsuki idenu,
Katsura Gawa tsuki no akaki ni zo
wataru.   Hito-bito no iwaku.   Kono,
kawa Asuka Gawa ni araneba, fuchi se
sara ni kawarazari keri to iite, aru hito
no yomeru uta,

Hisakata no
Tsuki ni oitaru

23 MAR. 16th *day.*—That evening, as he went up to the Capital, he saw in the shops at Yamasaki the little boxes painted with pictures and the rice-cakes twisted into the shape of conch shells, just the same as ever ; and he wondered if the hearts of the shopkeepers also were the same.[66] After this, on the road to the Capital, many people, and not necessarily his own relations, entertained him at Shimasaka. Indeed, they were more hospitable on his return than when he set out, and in some way or other he would have liked to make some return for it. Planning to arrive at the Capital by night, he did not hasten. The moon had risen, and he crossed the Katsura River in bright moonlight. Every one said that as this was not the Asuka River,[67] it would not suddenly change itself to eddies and rapids ; and ' a certain personage ' composed this :

> 'Neath the moon of heaven
> Flows the River Katsura

Katsura Kawa
Soko naru kage mo
Kawarazari keri.

Mata, aru hito no ieru.

Ama-gumo no
Haruka nari-tsuru
Katsura Kawa
Sode wo hidete mo
Watari nuru kana.

Mata, aru hito no yomeru.

Katsura Kawa
Waga kokoro ni mo
Kayowanedo
Onaji fukasa ni
Nagaru-bera nari.

Miyako no ureshiki amari ni, uta
mo amari zo ōkaru. Yo fukete ku-
reba, tokoro-dokoro miezu. Miyako ni

Slowly growing old ;
In its depths the moon lies low
As it did long, long ago.[68]

He recited this also :

Once Katsura's Stream
Seemed to me as far away
    As the clouds of heaven ;
Now, while crossing, I perceive
It has wet my dipping sleeve.

And again he composed this :

Well I know my heart
And the River Katsura
    Never were alike ;
Yet in depth my heart would seem
Not unlike the flowing stream.

These too many verses are due to his excessive pleasure at reaching the Capital. The night was growing late and some places could not be seen, but it was delightful to enter the Capital once more.

iri-tachite ureshi. Ie ni itarite. Kado
ni iru ni, tsuki aka-kereba, ito yoku
arisama miyu. Kikishi yori mo masa-
rite, iu kainaku zo, kobore yaburetaru.
Ie wo azuketari-tsuru hito no, kokoro
mo aretaru nari keri. Naka-kaki koso
are. Hitotsu ie no yō nareba, nozomite
azukareru nari. Sareba, tayori goto ni,
mono mo taezu esasetaru. Koyoi kakaru koto to, kowadaka ni mono mo
iwasezu. Ito wa tsuraku miyuredo, kokoro-
zashi wa sen to su. Sate ike meite
kubomari, mizu keru tokoro ari. Hotori ni matsu mo ariki, itsutose, mutose
no uchi ni, chitose ya sugi ni ken, katae
wa nakunari ni keri. Ima oitaru zo
majireru. Ōkata, mina are nitareba,

On reaching his home and entering his
door, the moon was so bright that he
could see the state of things at a glance.
Needless to say the whole place was
hopelessly overgrown and ragged, even
more than he had been told ! The heart
of the man, to whom he had entrusted his
home, must be as waste as it ! Their
two houses, separated only by a hedge,
looked as if they were both one, so he had
hopefully left it in his charge, and had
never failed to send him a present on every
opportunity. Well, that evening he
determined he would not speak about it
in a loud tone of voice ; and, though he
felt very angry, he had to make some sort
of acknowledgement. Then, again, the
ground had sunk and was full of water, as
if it was a pond. There was a pine tree
close by, and it had overgrown in five or
six years, as if in a thousand years ; half
its branches were dead, and the young
growing ones all in confusion. Almost

aware to zo hito-bito iu. Omoi-idenu koto naku, koishiki ga uchi ni, kono ie nite umareshi joshi no, morotomo ni kaeraneba, ikaga wa kanashiki. Funa-bito-domo, mina, ko idakite nonoshiru, kakaru uchi ni, nao kanashimi ni taezu shite, hisoka ni, kokoro shireru hito to ieri keru uta,

> Umareshi mo
> Kaeranu mono wo
> Waga yado ni
> Ko-matsu no aru wo
> Miru ga kanashisa.

To zo ieru. Nao, akazu ya aran. Mata, kaku nan.

> Mishi hito wo
> Matsu no chitose ni
> Mi-mashikaba

everything was the same, and everybody
offered him their sympathy. He recalled
especially how his little daughter had been
born in that house, in its beloved interior;
how sad it was that she had not returned
with them ! The sailors and others were
talking loudly as they embraced their
children, and just then his grief was more
than he could bear; so to one who
sympathized with his feelings he softly
whispered this verse :

> Never to return.
> To our home where she was born ;
>   Ah, how pitiful !
> Yet the pine tree shoots live on,
> Though our little girl is gone.

Thus he spoke. And if that is not
enough, here is yet one more :

> Could I have endowed
> With the pine tree's thousand years
>   One I used to see,

Tōku kanashiki
Wakarese-mashi ya.

Wasure-gataku kuchi-oshiki koto ōkaredo, tsukusazu. Tomare kakumare, toku
yariten.

Parted from her nevermore
All my sorrows would be o'er.

His sorrows, which he can never forget,
are more than he can ever express. Well,
well,—this must be torn up at once.

NOTES

1

As explained in the Introduction, this opening sentence means that the diary is to be written in 'the women's language', i.e. in phonetic characters only, without the use of ideographs; and, in order to be consistent, Tsurayuki writes as if he was a woman, and mentions himself only in the third person, using different names, such as 'a certain personage', 'the seafarer', &c.

2

29 JAN. *Uma no hanamuke* means to 'turn your horse's nose', which was an old expression corresponding to our 'stirrup cup'; it gradually came to mean any kind of farewell present made to one about to start on a journey. In this case it evidently took the form of *saké*, and Tsurayuki himself notices how incongruous the expression is for one about to travel by sea. Elsewhere I have translated it simply 'to make a farewell present'.

3

29 JAN. Salt is generally used to preserve food, and one would therefore naturally expect it to preserve the travellers; but here we find them, by the side of a whole ocean of salt water, *azare*, literally 'gŏne bad' —like tainted meat or fish.

4

31 JAN. This refers to the staggering footprints of the intoxicated sailors on the shore. They were illiterate men, unable to form a single ideographic character; but Tsurayuki noticed that their feet had unconsciously made the character for ' ten ', which is similar to our sign for plus. An alternative reading is that they staggered in ten different directions; for *tomoji*, if written in phonetics only as the original was, would give both meanings. There seems to be another play upon words here also; for *ashi wa, to-*, if read as one word *ashiato*, means ' footprints '.

5

1 FEB. This is the official residence of the Governor of Tosa, recently occupied by Tsurayuki, but now given up to his successor, the new Governor.

6

2 FEB. The Chinese poems are not given, because the writer, in his assumed rôle of a woman, would not be supposed to understand them or be able to write them down. This same expression *Kara uta*, or Chinese poem, is frequently used elsewhere in the diary, meaning nothing more than ' classical verse ', i.e. the *tanka*, of which so many examples are given.

7

3 FEB. This was a little girl, nine years of age, who had been born in Kyōto, the Capital, and who accompanied her father to Tosa on his appointment to the Governorship. She had recently died, and her parents were inconsolable for her loss.

8

3 FEB. That is, a brother of the newly appointed Governor.

9

3 FEB. *Oshi* means 'regret', as I have translated it, but it also suggests *oshi-dori* (mandarin ducks), which, as a symbol of happy married life, might refer to Tsurayuki and his wife; while *ashi kamo* (the ducks among the reeds) are the friends who have come to bid farewell.

10

3 FEB. This steersman, who acts as captain of the ship, is a character of great interest to Tsurayuki, who continually mentions him in the course of his diary.

11

3 FEB. *Kai-uta* can mean either 'a song of the East' or 'a song of the sea', and probably both meanings are intended here. The Province of Kōshū, which lies to the east of the Capital, Kyōto, is also called *Kai*. *Sai-Koku*, the Land of the West, refers to the Province of Tosa, because it lies west of Kyōto. The dust blowing about in the cabin and the clouds scudding across the sky are supposed to be agitated by the beauty of the songs they have just heard sung.

12

3 FEB. These two faithful friends, Fujiwara no Tokisané and Tachibana no Suehira, follow the departing Governor to Ōminato, the last spot in Tosa Province at which the boat stops, and bid him a final farewell ten days later.

13

5 FEB. The doctor's present was to enable the travellers to celebrate the New Year with all due honours. Spiced *saké* was then drunk to ensure long life. *Byakusan* (lit. ' white powder ') was, according to the dictionaries, a composition of Japanese pepper, cassia, campanula, and *atractylis ovata*, of which some parts, probably the roots or seeds, were dried, ground up small, mixed together, and added to the *saké*.

14

6 FEB. These references are all to the customs and ceremonies of the New Year. Potatoes were eaten then, to imply a wish that your family might be as numerous as the potatoes on one plant. Seaweed was a symbol of good luck, and is supposed to refer to the recorded fact that when the Empress Jingō was about to embark with her armies for the subjugation of Korea in the year A.D. 202, her horses ran short of fodder ; so she caused them to be fed on seaweed, which so refreshed and invigorated them that she secured a complete victory. Rice-cakes, made in the form of a mirror, were supposed to harden the teeth if eaten at the New Year, and mullet heads were sucked, it is said, to express a wish that you might be the head of a family. Tsurayuki had no mullets (*nayoshi*), but he had one trout (*oshiayu*), the names of which are not very dissimilar in the original ; so the ship's company did the best they could by sucking it in turn, a process which evidently struck the writer as very disgusting. His thoughts turned longingly to Kyōto, where the New Year was being celebrated in a proper manner. The straw rope with tufts of straw or cut paper at intervals was hung over the doors of houses at the New Year ; it commemorated the straw rope hung across the mouth of the cave in the time of the Gods, which prevented the Sun Goddess from retiring again, after she had been enticed out.

15

12 FEB. *Ao Uma* is literally a blue (or green) horse, i.e. a grey horse. On the seventh day of the first month ten sacred grey horses, which were kept at a temple in Kyōto, were solemnly paraded before the Emperor, while priestesses performed a sacred dance. Tsurayuki regrets that he can only see white waves now, when he would much rather be watching the parade of the grey horses.

16

12 FEB. *Iké* means a pond or pool, and one would naturally expect carp to come from an estate bearing that name ; but the writer says the present consisted of nearly every other kind of fish, but not carp.

17

12 FEB. *Wakana*, green vegetables or young green shoots, were always picked on the seventh day of the first month.

18

12 FEB. *Warawa* means a child, and there is nothing in the text to say whether it was a boy or a girl. But the Kōgi edition, which I have used, adds in a note that it was probably the latter, because in the *Gosenshū* (a collection of poetry) there is a verse attributed to a daughter of Tsurayuki, who might therefore be this child.

19

13 FEB. The original verse by Ariwara no Narihira, who lived A.D. 825–80, is found in the Seventeenth Book of the *Kokinshū*, and runs :

Akanaku ni
Madaki mo tsuki no

Kakururu ka
Yama no ha nigete
Irezu mo aranan.

Now the lovely moon,
Though I fain would watch it still,
    Hides away from sight.
Would the hills but fly away
Longer might the moonlight stay.

20

13 FEB. The River of the Sky is the Japanese name for the Milky Way; the moon is supposed to be floating on it like a boat. Ōminato, where they have been detained ever since the twenty-eighth day of the previous month, means 'the great harbour', and Tsurayuki no doubt refers to this in the verse (*izuru minato* = leaving port).

21

14 FEB. A pine tree is reputed to live for a thousand years, and both it and the stork are emblems of long life.

22

14 FEB. This very irregular composition seems to be a kind of folk-song. *Shūtome* in the seventh line is really a 'mother-in-law', and not 'mother', as I have given it.

23

14 FEB. These are Tsurayuki and his wife, who are suffering from sea-sickness, which attacked all the passengers this day, and which was no doubt the reason of their not travelling on the following day.

24

16 FEB. *Hané* means the wing or feathers of a bird.

25

16 FEB. The whole verse is to be found in the Ninth Book of the *Kokinshū*, where it is stated to be by an unknown writer. A husband and wife journeyed together to a distant part of the country, where the husband died, and the sorrowing wife retraced her steps alone to the Capital. On the journey a flock of wild geese passed her with mournful cries as they flew north again after wintering in warm climates, and she then composed this verse. It runs:

> Kita e yuku
> Kari zo nakunaru
> Tsurete koshi
> Kazu wa tarade zo
> Kaeru-bera naru.

> Wild geese heading north
> With a sad and mournful cry,
> Whom do you lament?
> Was there in the flock last year
> One who does not reappear?

26

16 FEB. Note the three long lines in the original all beginning with *omoi* (thought, care, anxiety), which I have tried in vain to reproduce in the translation.

27

18 FEB. They evidently took advantage of some one of the natural hot-springs in the neighbourhood, of which there are so many in Japan.

28

18 FEB. The God of the Sea, jealous of such a blaze of wealth and beauty, might have brought destruction upon the ship. The words within brackets are unsuited for translation.

29

20 FEB. Rice and bean gruel used to be eaten on the first, fifteenth, and twenty-eighth days of the month, which is probably the reason why the writer mentions its omission on this occasion. As it was an inauspicious day for travelling, they might have courted disaster if they had moved at their usual rate.

30

21 FEB. This is hardly correct. It was twenty-five days since he left his official residence, but he spent six days in feasting before he really started.

31

22 FEB. The Japanese say that they see a *katsura* bush growing on the face of the moon.

32

22 FEB. Possibly both these verses are by Tsurayuki, for both are attributed to *aru hito* (a certain personage) ; but the Kōgi edition, which I have used, offers no opinion about it.

33

22 FEB. The word I have translated 'ship's officers' is the plural of *kajitori*, a steersman, which is generally used here for the captain of the ship. The plural form occurs again on the second of March.

34

23 FEB. 'The venerable master of the ship' is no doubt intended for Tsurayuki himself, although the Kōgi edition suggests as an alternative that it means the steersman. His gloomy thoughts perhaps refer to the death of his little daughter, to which he constantly makes allusion. In the following verse he combines both the similes expressed in his former attempts.

35

23 FEB. As explained in the Introduction, the *tanka* or short verse was limited to thirty-one syllables.

36

25 FEB. Abe no Naka Maro was one of the greatest of the old poets, he died in the year A.D. 780. He had been sent on a mission to China, some say to discover the secret of the Chinese calendar, and he composed the verse which follows at a farewell banquet in the year A.D. 726, just before he started on his way home to Japan.

37

25 FEB. This well-known verse is included in the anthology called *Hyaku Nin Isshū*; but there the first line is given as *Ama no hara*, which would change the translation to ' I, while gazing up, far into the heav'nly sky '. The Temple of Kasuga was near Nara, Naka Maro's home, and the verse expresses his feelings of home-sickness.

38

25 FEB. The Chinese, of course, would not understand the Japanese spoken language when they heard the verse recited, but when written in their own ideographic characters it would be perfectly plain to them.

39

26 FEB. This is the boat song as given, but there are two syllables too many for a *tanka* verse, and it is hard to discover any metre in it.

40

26 FEB. Tsurayuki as Governor had had to dispense justice to these pirates, and they had threatened to take their revenge if they caught him at sea. He is afraid that they may now take him at a disadvantage if they meet him, for the sea is getting rough. His hair almost turns white with fear; but, as he says, dangers are so common at sea that it is only what one must expect.

41

3 MAR. These *nusa*, or *gohei* as they are generally called now, are pieces of white paper cut in a particular shape. Originally they represented votive offerings of pure white silk or cloth, and they are generally to be seen at Shintō Temples.

42

3 MAR. This is one of Tsurayuki's attendants, possibly his housekeeper, who was, no doubt, a native of Awaji Island.

43

3 MAR. *Hote uchite* is supposed to mean 'hoisting sail', taking *hote* as a contraction for *ho no te* or *hozuna*, 'a halyard'.

44

4 MAR. A possible second meaning of this verse would be :

> Loud the tempests roar,
> Not an instant dying down,
>   And the waves arise.
> Up and down the billows will
> Make our journey longer still.

This would necessitate reading *nami-ji* as two words (when the waves arise our road becomes longer and longer).

45

4 MAR. To snap the fingers was to ward off bad luck, in this case in the hope of making the wind die down.

46

6 MAR. Instead of our week the Japanese used to use the Chinese twelve-day period, each day being called after one of the Signs of the Zodiac, of which the Rat was the first. The first Rat Day of the year, or *Ne no Hi*, was always kept as a holiday, when the proper thing to do was to go out and pick the fresh green sprouts of early spring, and pull up young pine-tree shoots to ensure a long life.

47

6 MAR. *Umi-matsu*, literally 'sea-pine', is a name for coral. The idea is that a fisherwoman, being on the sea for the Day of the Rat, would do the best she could to pluck up a young pine by diving for coral (sea-pine).

48

6 MAR. Possibly this woman may be intended for Tsurayuki himself, the former Governor of Tosa, in his character of a female writer. Or it may be his wife or one of his suite to whom he refers.

49

8 MAR. The five primary colours, according to the Japanese, are black, white, red, blue (or green), and yellow.

50

8 MAR. *Tamakushige* is a conventional poetical epithet, meaning 'like a box of pearls', here very aptly used, for Hako no Ura, the place they were passing, means 'Casket Beach'.

51

10 MAR. *Tama* means a pearl or jewel, or when used with *namida* (tears) it means teardrops. This verse is a play upon the double meaning; if only his teardrops were real pearls, he would preserve them by stringing them on a thread.

52

11 MAR. *Wasure-gai*, literally 'forgetting-shell', is a black and grey clam shell, often mentioned in old Japanese poetry. Its signification is the exact opposite of our forget-me-not flower. The writer of this verse is supposed to have been Tsurayuki's wife, the mother of his dead child.

53

11 MAR. This is a play upon the word Izumi, the name of the Province on whose shores they were camping, which means 'a spring of water'. I have had to use the word twice to bring out the meaning in the translation.

54

12 MAR. *Imo ga umu* is a conventional poetical epithet meaning 'like a maiden spinning'. It is used here with Ozu, because *o* is the word for 'thread'. But, as a matter of fact, *o* in this case means 'little', for Ozu is 'the little harbour'.

55

12 MAR. See Introduction for a note on the *tanka* metre. The *ō* in *ōse-tabu* counts as two syllables.

56

12 MAR. Suminoye and Sumiyoshi are one and the same place.

57

12 MAR. *Wasure-gusa* (forgetting-grass) is an old word for reeds or rushes, which seem to have grown in great profusion about Naniwa and Suminoye. The name is used in the same sense as the forgetting-shells mentioned in the entry for the previous day.

58

12 MAR. The old Japanese mirror was made of bronze with a highly polished face, and a back generally elaborately decorated.

59

12 MAR. This sly cut at the steersman shows that Tsurayuki, who was genuinely distressed at the loss of his mirror, was sceptical about the God of Suminoye.

60

13 MAR. *Miotsukushi* means 'a tide gauge'. It was set up off the port of Naniwa, and is frequently mentioned in old Japanese poetry.

61

15 MAR. A note in the Kōgi edition says that this chronic complaint was some disease of old age ; otherwise one would have thought it might have had reference to the remains of his attack of sea-sickness, from which he had not yet recovered. 'To fish with a grain of rice' is equivalent to our expression 'to fish with a sprat for a whale'.

62

16 MAR. This verse by Ariwara no Narihira is to be found in the First Book of the *Kokinshū*.

63

16 MAR. *Furu*, in the second line, has a double meaning. If taken with *yado*, it means 'an old (house)'; but if taken with *yo wo*, it means '(the blossoms) spend (their lives, &c.)'.

64

18 MAR. Hachiman is the God of War.

65

21 MAR. *Kuruma* here does not mean a jinrikisha, which is a modern innovation of the nineteenth century.

66

23 MAR. Does this hint that Tsurayuki had on a former occasion found the shopkeepers not quite honest?

67

23 MAR. The Asuka River, notorious for sudden spates and rapids, was as uncertain as its name, which, read as *asu ka*, means ' Who knows what the morrow will bring ? '

68

23 MAR. A second meaning is that the *katsura* bush, which is supposed to be visible on the face of the moon, is growing old, but still the moon's reflection in the Katsura River remains the same.